You're Not Much Use to Anyone

You're Not Much Use to Anyone

David Shapiro

New Harvest
Houghton Mifflin Harcourt
BOSTON • NEW YORK
2014

This edition published by special arrangement with Amazon Publishing

Amazon and the Amazon logo are trademarks of Amazon.com, Inc. or its affiliates.

For information about permission to reproduce selections from this book,
go to www.apub.com.

www.hmhco.com

Library of Congress Cataloging-in-Publication Data
Shapiro, David
You're not much use to anyone : a novel / David Shapiro
pages cm. — (New Harvest)
ISBN 978-0-544-26230-0 (hardback)
I. Title.
PS3619.H35593Y69 2014
813'.6 — dc23
2014001291

Printed in the United States of America
DOC 10 9 8 7 6 5 4 3 2 1

Dedicated to people who will read it slowly

You're Not Much Use to Anyone

1

Me and Camilla walk uptown from the East Village, where we spent the afternoon, to Camilla's friend Emma's parents' apartment on the Upper West Side because Emma is visiting from college in Pennsylvania, and her parents aren't home. It's 2008 and I'm twenty.

As we're walking, Camilla looks down at her legs and says, "I think my legs will never be skinny. Like, I think if I starved to death, I would look like a skeleton except with fat legs, you know?"

"I don't think that's true," I say, but I know what she means.

Camilla has been trying to set me up with someone and she thinks I'll like Emma. We walk through the East 20s, and Camilla says Emma is hot and that when they were in high school, Emma got way more attention from boys than she did. We walk up to the discount liquor store on 29th Street and Third, and Camilla says I should get the liquor because my fake ID is better than hers. She gives me a twenty and smokes while I buy vodka. I come out, and as we walk, she tells me about how when she and Emma went to boarding school in the mountains in Colorado, they both liked a boy who was two years younger than they were, and who once asked them to kiss each other and how they did it, and then the three of them all kissed simultaneously. Camilla giggles and says, "He was a city kid, so it seemed like he was older."

I tell Camilla I hope that someday I can be involved in a three-way kiss, and she shrugs and says that it doesn't seem like it's out of the realm of possibility. I say, "I've mostly only had long-term girlfriends, and those are the people who it's hardest to propose three-way kisses to, you know?" Camilla shrugs again and says that it depends on the girlfriend. Then we pass an ad for a new flavor of Doritos, and Camilla takes a picture of it with her BlackBerry and sends it to Mike, my roommate, who Camilla started dating after I introduced them. They're both enthusiastic about processed food. Her BlackBerry background is the Doritos logo, but it says "Don'tEatThose" inside the logo where it usually says "Doritos."

On the way, I wash my face in a Starbucks bathroom. It's humid and I've been sweating and I don't want to appear greasy. We get to Emma's building, and the doorman calls up to her apartment and lets us through. Camilla fixes her hair in the elevator, using the two-way mirror that covers the security camera. Mike texts her back and she smiles.

2

Emma opens the door, hugs Camilla, and says, really tenderly, "How are you doing?" She draws out the word "doing" until the "ooh" sounds like a musical note. Camilla tells her how she's doing, which is pretty good. Then Emma shakes my hand, and she and Camilla talk as I mostly stay quiet and stand behind Camilla. There are some other kids drinking and talking in the living room. Emma has big boobs and long brown hair. Her face is perfectly shaped. She offers me a beer from her fridge. I take it and then excuse myself to go to the bathroom and wash my face again, and when I come back, I sit down on the couch in the living room next to some kid wearing cargo shorts who's sitting with his legs splayed out, so there's not much room for me to sit. He doesn't move, and so I squeeze in next to him and introduce myself, and he looks exactly like Emma so I'm sure he's Emma's brother. He looks older than me and looks unfriendly, but this is the best open seat in the apartment with respect to the TV.

I ask him where his parents are and he says, "On vacation," and then I try to talk to him about *Seinfeld*, both because it's on and because it's my favorite show. "Did you know Jerry's apartment is actually like five blocks from where we are right now?" I ask. "It's on 81st between Amsterdam and Columbus. And people all over the country and the world are watching *Seinfeld* right now, but we're among the closest people to where his apartment actually is. I mean closest among people who are currently watching the show. That's kind of cool to think about, I think."

"That's not true."

"What do you mean?"

"Jerry Seinfeld's apartment is on 81st Street and Central Park West."

"No, but I meant his fictional apartment in the show, not his real apartment in life . . ."

Emma's brother doesn't look at me or respond so I excuse myself to go to the bathroom to get away from him, and as I'm getting up he says, "Didn't you just come from the bathroom?" I tell him that I just washed my face and he goes, "Did you use our family's hand towels on your face?" I tell him I used toilet paper to dry my face, and he looks at me like he doesn't believe me.

3

I find Camilla again, and she says that she and Emma are going up to the roof to smoke and that I should come. I whisper, "Her brother was really weird to me for no reason," and Camilla says, "Really? He's always nice to me . . . ?" I say, "You're a girl. Obviously he's nice to you." Camilla thinks about this and nods.

Ten minutes later, me and Camilla and Emma and a disinterested-seeming blond girl sit at a picnic table and smoke and pour the liquor that I bought into glasses of Diet Coke. The picnic table has benches welded to it, and me and Camilla sit opposite Emma and the disinterested blond girl. Emma thanks us for the liquor and I say, "Yeah, of course," and then she points to the bottle, which is a bottle of vodka called Cîroc, and says, "Why'd you get this one though? Isn't this like the P. Diddy vodka?" I'd kind of hoped she'd ask me something like this because I have some good canned conversation about Cîroc.

I say, "Yeah, it is the P. Diddy vodka, but also it's actually the only vodka made of grapes, and you can sort of taste the grapes a little. It's hard to taste distinctions among vodkas but this one is really distinct. Can you taste the grapes?"

Emma takes a sip and thinks for a second and nods hesitantly and says, "Sort of." The blond girl lights another cigarette and doesn't take a sip of her vodka.

I say, "And also there's an ad campaign for this vodka with a

5

black-and-white picture of Diddy sitting at a very formal-seeming dinner table, wearing a tuxedo and surrounded by people wearing tuxedos and formal gowns, and he's holding a Cîroc-based drink in one hand, like a martini, but Diddy's wearing a huge pair of sunglasses, which look out of place. Because he's at a formal dinner party, surrounded by people in tuxedos. At the dinner table."

Emma and Camilla look at me quizzically. I go, "Nobody who's actually attending a really formal dinner party would wear huge glasses with dark lenses like that indoors, you know? It's impolite, like wearing a hat at the table. And it would be hard for him to see."

Nobody says anything. Maybe they'd have to see the ad to understand. Or maybe I just should never have said anything. My story didn't really have a point or a punch line. I'm not going to tell that one again, ever. It wasn't even really a story. The blond girl says she's gonna leave but it was nice to meet me.

4

Emma and Camilla reminisce about boarding school in the woods in Colorado. They tell me that they had to live in cabins and tents and go on nature hikes and runs, but it was really hard to run because the air was so thin up in the mountains. I say, "One time I had a two-hour plane layover at the airport in Denver so I know what you mean," and Emma laughs, so I pretend I was joking.

Camilla gets up from the table to take a phone call and leaves me with Emma, and Emma asks me to tell her secret stuff or gossip about Camilla that Camilla wouldn't say herself.

I say, "I'm not sure of what Camilla would or wouldn't tell you so I don't really know what kind of stuff you're trying to find out." I try not to stare at Emma's boobs or say anything weird. I just wish she would talk about herself, so I say, "How do you like school?" She starts talking and I nod along.

Even though it's nighttime, I can still see clouds in the sky because they're lit up by the city lights. I'm starting to sweat again, and Emma notices and says, "It's hot out here, right?" and I go, "It's not the heat, it's the humidity," which is a reference to a movie or a TV show, I think, but I can't remember what, and she smiles. Then a dude with a sleeve of tattoos and a skateboard and a Supreme hat comes up to us and sits down on the bench next to her and puts his arm around her and introduces himself.

5

A year and a half later, on a night in December, I finish my last exam in my last class of my last semester of college. I walk out of the building and light a cigarette to celebrate. I don't usually smoke cigarettes, but I feel like I should do something to mark the occasion. In front of the MLB Fan Cave on 4th Street, where there are two guys watching a lot of different baseball games on screens, I call my grandma and say, "Hey, Bubba. I finished college," and she congratulates me and tells me she's sending me a check, which is good because it will allow me to not ask my parents for extra money on top of my monthly rent check, at least this month. She asks me about my postgraduate plans, and I tell her that I finished one semester early because I took the minimum number of credits I needed to get my degree and my dad said there was no reason to stay at school after that. And so, because I finished early and saved my parents a semester's worth of tuition, I have like five months of leeway before I have to begin productive adulthood. "But what will you do with your time?" she says, and I tell her that I'll figure it out. "I have an economics degree now, so maybe something with that?" I add. "I don't really know. I'll probably go to law school or something." Mostly what I want to do is ride my bike and take Klonopin, but obviously it's hard to parlay those activities into lucrative careers.

I get home and read the classifieds on Craigslist, but there's nothing appealing and I don't think I could get any of the jobs anyway. Even though they're all administrative or secretarial or something, they probably have like five hundred overqualified applicants already applying to them. Then my mom calls to congratulate me on graduating. She wants to assess the seriousness of my job search, and I tell her that if I were a gun and résumés and cover letters were bullets, I would be an automatic rifle that shoots sixty bullets a minute. I say, "And my friends are like those Revolutionary War muskets that you have to clean out every time you fire them." She tells me to send her my résumé so she can look it over, and once she seems satisfied with my determination to get a job, she tells me that she's going to transfer a thousand dollars into my bank account at the end of the month.

Then my dad gets on the phone and asks if I want them to come to my official graduation ceremonies at Radio City Music Hall and Yankee Stadium. It doesn't really matter to me, which I tell him, and he sounds relieved and says that my mom thought I would want to go to those graduations, but he knows that I know that it's "bullshit pomp circumstance — everyone graduates from college in this country! Why do we need a big ceremony every time someone graduates?" This is actually a sentiment I agree with, I guess, so I don't protest.

He asks how old I think I'll be when he stops supporting me. "Hopefully exactly the same age I am now," I say, and he laughs like that's a ridiculous supposition, and then my mom, who has been listening in on our conversation the whole time, tells him not to be cruel, and he yells at her for listening in on his private conversation, and then she apologizes and hangs up for real this time.

To prevent my dad from asking me more questions, I ask

what he's been up to. He says he's reading an important article on 321gold.com about how the Chinese government is buying all of the gold in America to precipitate the decline of the dollar and deliberately impoverish the United States, and then promises to send me a link. The last time he sent me a link it was about how the heads of major banks are all Illuminati puppets, and I think about how much of whatever he's about to send me I'll have to read to convince him that I read the whole thing. Probably just the headline.

After we talk for a few more minutes about the upcoming New World Order and the Illuminati-orchestrated collapse of the dollar and this country's lack of a future and the fact that we should all leave and move to a country that has a future, I tell my dad I have to get back to writing cover letters and he lets me go. I'm hungry, so I buy a Clif Bar at a bodega and eat it on the street while I walk to Camilla's.

6

At Camilla's, I take a bottle of kombucha out of the fridge and sit down on the couch with her. She's watching Bravo and says, suggestively, "Emma's coming over in a few minutes, and she's staying over in Shira's room because Shira's on a family trip." I ask if Emma's single, and Camilla says that she is, and I say, "You said that last time and then there was that guy with the Supreme hat," and Camilla says, "Well, as far as I know, right now, she's single, and you can take that information and do with it what you please," so I go into the bathroom to wash my face and comb my hair with my hand. I come back into the living room and Camilla says, "How's Mike?" and I say, "He's fine. He's home right now, I think." She waits a second and says, "He can really go fuck himself. Is he still with that fat girl? Why did he ever even pretend he cared about me?" I say, "I don't know if I should become involved in this," and she says, "Can you just listen?"

She complains about Mike and then Emma gets there. She and Camilla hug, and then she and I hug. We each look at the other's face for what seems like a second longer than necessary and then I avert my eyes. Five minutes later I'm sitting between Emma and Camilla on the couch, and the two of them are talking about what's going on in the Bravo show and also about their plans for winter break. To graduate on time, Emma has to take classes during Winter Session, while Camilla is doing the same thing I'm doing, which is thinking about what she's gonna be when she grows up. She still has another semester. Emma asks me what I've been up to and I say, "I graduated college, pending the results of my behavioral economics exam."

"Oh, when was that?" she says.

"Four and a half hours ago."

"So you're four and a half hours into adulthood," Camilla says.

"I get a temporary stay of adulthood because I graduated early," I say.

"If you go to grad school, you could reset the clock on adulthood for years," Emma half jokes.

7

We start watching *200 Cigarettes* and drinking Bud Lights. Emma's jeans, I notice, are made of a stretchy material, and they don't have pockets or a fly, and I envision her standing naked on a huge half shell that's suspended on a wave. By the time I'm done describing the plot of *200 Cigarettes* up to the point in the movie where we are, Camilla has fallen asleep and her head is slumped over the arm of the couch. Emma looks at her and whispers, "Do you wanna go into Shira's room?" I ask her, "Why?" And she gives me an indecipherable look for a second and then says, "We don't have to go," and I say, "No, we can go, I was just wondering why?" She looks at me blankly so I say, "Actually, never mind . . . We, like, shouldn't wake Camilla up if she's sleeping."

So we walk quietly into Shira's room, and Emma closes the door and sits down on the side of Shira's bed, and Emma picks up a copy of *Cosmopolitan* off the nightstand and opens it and starts flipping through it. We're sitting right next to each other, our legs touching, ostensibly so we can both read the magazine easily, but it feels like maybe there's something else going on. But I'm not sure yet. "Do you want to do one of the quizzes?" Emma asks.

"Maybe we should do the quiz together. It'll be boring for you if I take a teenage girl quiz and you're just sitting there."

"What if we have different answers?"

I say, "I think we'd be able to reach a consensus."

After the quiz, Emma picks up another teen girl magazine and we go through that one too. Her hands are small and look soft. She laughs at some of the things I say and brushes my leg and arm with her small, soft hand sometimes, and then I look up at the clock and it's later than I thought it was. Emma looks at it too, and I feel like she's probably presenting the opportunity for me to make a move here, and maybe has been for the last half hour, and if I don't do it soon, this will get weirder than it should have been. So I go to the bathroom to wash my face and then come back and sit down on the other side of her. It's easier for me to kiss her from this side, and I put my hand up to her face and start kissing her, and she kisses back. I get that rush of good feelings.

We kiss on the side of the bed for about five minutes, and then she pulls away and we look at each other for like two or three seconds. She breathes a little and her breath smells good. Emma smiles a little bit and excuses herself to go to the bathroom. I hold my hand in front of my face and breathe softly against my palm. It smells okay. Then Emma comes back and turns the light off and pushes me down onto Shira's bed and gets on top of me, and we start making out again, and I feel like a fourteen-year-old whose older sister's friend is introducing him to manhood.

She takes her shirt off, then my shirt off, and I suck in my stomach the most that it could possibly be sucked in without her noticing that's what I'm doing. Ten minutes later, we take our pants off and get under the covers. Emma starts sliding down the bed like she's about to go down on me, but I stop her because I know that if she does that I'll come in like forty-five seconds, so I go down on her and she seems like she's uncomfortable at first but then she starts to appear to like it. Then I come accidentally, with almost no physical provocation, which is pretty embarrassing if she noticed. This makes me think about how I have to get Shira's sheets washed tomorrow because I came in her bed, but then Emma seems like she comes too, and she makes a noise to indicate that she's content. I slide up next to her and put my arm around her and she starts to reach down toward my underwear, and I say, "No, it's fine, I'm fine . . ." She looks at me. I can't generate a reasonable lie about why I wouldn't want her to do this so I tell her the truth. "I actually came."

We each go to the bathroom and then lie in bed with the lights off, with her arm across my chest and her head on my shoulder.

"Why don't you have a boyfriend?" I ask. Emma moves over and lies on her back, facing the ceiling, and her boobs are splayed out, like pointing in different directions. Very white. She thinks for a second and goes, "I go to an all-girls school. You're the only boy I've met in months." I ask her what happened to the boy with the Supreme hat and she says, "We don't talk." Then she thinks about what she's said and goes, "But not in a pointed way. Like, we're not *not* talking. We just don't really have anything to say to each other, you know?" I nod and try to smell her hair without her noticing.

The next morning, Emma has to go back to school, so I walk her to the subway. We stand in front of the subway entrance and I talk nervously, just to keep her there, because I'm not sure if it would be inappropriate to kiss her because we just hooked up one time and a public kiss might violate her understanding of the boundaries of our relationship at this point, but then I do it anyway and she kisses back, but it's more of a peck. She gives me her phone number and goes into the subway and then I go back to Camilla's and take Shira's sheets to the laundry.

8

Two weeks later, me and Mike are sitting around in the living room. I'm reading Pitchfork album reviews and complaining about them, and he's touring different cities on Google Maps Street View. He shows me how parts of Dubai look like an ancient desert, while other parts are like a futuristic city, and also how a lot of houses in Germany are blocked out on Street View because Germans are more serious about their privacy.

My mom calls.

"David, what are you doing right now?" she asks. She seems excited about something.

"I'm working on a cover letter for a research assistant job at a company that makes Greek yogurt," I tell her.

"David, you know you've told me that before? The Greek yogurt company? I think last time you told me you were applying for a marketing assistant job there."

"No way, this is the first time I've applied there."

"Okay, listen," she says after a long sigh. "Do you remember Linda, from my office?"

"Yeah, why?"

"Wait — why would a yogurt company need a research assistant? What would they research?"

"I don't know, new yogurt formulas . . . ?"

"But you don't have any sort of background in science."

"I took a class on the brain to fulfill my science requirement freshman year."

She pauses to take that in.

"Okay, well, Linda from my office took a job as general counsel for the Fire Department Pension Fund. And I told her you were looking for a job, and she said they're looking for someone at the Pension Fund, so I sent her your résumé yesterday, and she forwarded it to them, and they got back to her today and said they'd be happy to have you! Isn't that great?"

"Do you know what the job is?"

"Nope."

"Do you know the pay and the hours?"

"Whatever it is, it's more than you're making now!" She's laughing. "So you can hold off on applying for that research assistant position for the time being. They'll probably call you today!"

9

An hour later, I get a call from a Mr. Mangino who identifies himself as the director of Human Resources at the Fire Department Pension Fund. He tells me that my résumé looks good and that the job is twenty-five hours a week and that the pay is $20 an hour. I'll also get health care and other benefits associated with a full-time job, and there's a possibility that I will get a raise or be able to work full-time in the future, or maybe even, "with your qualifications, run the file room by yourself someday." I tell him I'll take the job because it doesn't seem like I have a choice or will be able to get another job. It's "a position in the file room," and he gives me the address of the office and tells me to be in the office on Monday at 9:30 for my orientation. Before we get off the phone, he suggests I send an Edible Arrangements bouquet to Linda Greenberg because I might be seeing her around the office a lot.

I call my mom and tell her that I got a job, and to tell my dad, and that the pay is around $400 a week, so she will still need to pay my rent but I can deal with my other expenses now. I tell her that the job is ideal because I can still have time to study for the LSAT after work.

Then I call Emma. We've texted occasionally since she left, and I made her a Belle and Sebastian mix and put it on Media-Fire and sent her the link. I checked my account two days later and the file had been downloaded — she was the only person I sent the link to, so I know she was the one who downloaded it. When I call, Emma is watering plants in a small indoor garden in one of the science buildings at her school.

"Can I come visit you?" I ask. "I got a job and I start on Monday."

"Ummm . . . When would you come?" She seems surprised.

"Today?"

She thinks about it for a second and asks if I know how to get to her school, and I tell her I could figure it out, and she says, nervously, "Okay, yeah, I guess that works?"

10

On the subway to Chinatown, and then on the Chinatown bus to Philadelphia, and then on the commuter train out to the college, I listen to Belle and Sebastian and think about how if the ten best tracks on Belle and Sebastian's 2005 B-sides and rarities collection *Push Barman to Open Old Wounds* were assembled onto one proper full-length album, it might possibly be better than *If You're Feeling Sinister*, their masterpiece. So I make On-The-Go playlists of different permutations of those ten tracks to create that album. I check Pitchfork to see what score *Push Barman* got and it's a 9.2 out of 10, which is really high. Usually the scores are way off, but at least they got that one right.

I stand outside the train station, which, after the train has left, is the most tranquil place I've stood in for months. Emma drives up and gets out of her car and stands next to it. She looks like she's just gotten out of the shower. I feel a wave of nervousness and walk up to her and say, "Hi," and put my hand up in a stationary wave. She says "Hi" back and steps in to hug me, and we stay in the hug for what feels like a long time but could just have been three seconds. I try to smell her hair without her noticing but she pulls away before I can get a good whiff. We get into her 1983 Oldsmobile, which has no CD or tape player. She seems a little embarrassed about having such a fat old car, but she shouldn't be embarrassed because I am impressed by anyone having a car. The floor is littered with empty water bottles and empty bags of Cheetos.

"You don't look like someone who eats a lot of Cheetos?" I say.

"I don't think people who eat Cheetos all have a certain look," Emma says.

There's a second of silence as I think of the next thing to say, but I eventually think of something and we make small talk as we drive to her dorm. We're both nervous, which I guess is better than if only I were nervous.

"So do you want to go to see what a real all-girls college party is like?" she asks as we sit at a red light.

"Shit, yeah," I say. "You think I'd come to an all-girls college and not expect to meet a ton of girls?" Emma doesn't say anything so I say, "I'm joking." Emma laughs and says, "I know," and so I say, "I only expect to meet like five girls," and Emma smiles and looks at me and then looks back at the road.

As we pull into the parking lot, there's another lull in our conversation, which makes me wonder if I made a mistake by coming here because maybe we don't have that much to talk about and don't have anything in common and this weekend is going to be a weird disaster, but then she asks me how my trip down was.

"It was okay," I tell her, "except there was a guy on the train who was holding a Bible and screaming about how a man isn't supposed to be with another man, and how there's nothing in the Bible about God loving everybody, and then he looked at me and yelled 'Faggot!' but I pretended I didn't hear him because I was wearing headphones."

"That sucks," she says.

"It got better once it seemed like he realized he couldn't break my headphone force field." She doesn't say anything so it seems wise for me to keep talking. "I wonder if people who preach on the subway specifically get on the subway and ride around to preach on it, or if they happen to be on the subway going somewhere already and they decide to start preaching?"

Emma parks the car, shifting a gear shifter that looks like a black dinosaur bone poking up out of the gearbox. We get out of the car and then kiss, then walk upstairs to her dorm room and have sex for a length of time that I'm proud of but do not care to reveal here. It isn't Herculean but I don't think she's disappointed.

11

We smoke old, dry weed that she keeps in a box on the floor under her bed, and I plug my iPod into her speakers so we can listen to Belle and Sebastian. I feel more relaxed. Emma decides to show me the garden she's growing in a building nearby, so we get dressed and walk out of her dorm. On the way there, we see two women walking together and holding hands under the lights that line the walkways around the quad. We walk into a building with 1970s architecture that looks like a prison, and Emma leads me to the room where she's growing her garden and tells me all about brassicas, which she's growing.

"Brassica is a genus of plant that has a ton of different edible species of plants under it," she says. "Mustard, broccoli, turnips, cabbage, cauliflower, even kohlrabi. It's crazy that all of those things are so genetically similar, right?" She sounds really passionate and tells me some other stuff about plants, and then she says she worked on an organic farm one summer in California and learned a lot about plants and farming. I tell her I'm on a crusade against organic fruit.

"Why?"

"It doesn't look as good as genetically modified fruit, it's puny, it bruises easily, it goes bad much more quickly, it's super expensive, it often doesn't taste as good, and if there was any serious health effect of eating genetically modified fruit, rather than just a generalized anxiety about how it's kind of freaky for fruits to look like they're on steroids, I think it would be illegal. Organic fruit is a racket."

She says, "It sounds like you have this memorized."

"Yeah, it's canned conversation, but I thought it was apropos of what you were saying."

Then I get really close to her and kiss her and put my hand on the back of her head, not in an aggressive way but in a gentle way, and we make out for like three or four minutes and then we water the plants she's growing and adjust the lights around them. I feel good around Emma, mostly because we had sex, so there's no lingering question about whether she will have sex with me or not.

12

On our walk from the plant building to the dorm where the party is, Emma lights a cigarette and says, "I'm worried about becoming addicted to cigarettes," and I ask her why she just doesn't smoke the one she's currently smoking, and she says, "Because I really want it. That's the issue." We get closer to the party and Emma holds my hand and says, "Okay, so, at this party, just watch out for this girl Erica. She's short and skinny and maybe will be wearing something, ummmm, revealing, and the last time we were at a party together she got drunk and said she wanted to sleep with me. So she might be weird to you."

"Like your brother?" I ask.

"No, not exactly like my brother. He's weird in a different way." She thinks for a second and says, "Actually, maybe sort of like that. But she's more aggressive."

I ask Emma if Erica is a lesbian and Emma says, "No, but it's just girls here, so, you know . . ."

She also tells me about a couple at this party, Ellie and Michelle, who are both straight but agreed to date each other until they graduate college. Then we get to the dorm building, and one of Emma's friends, a boy named Ryan who was born into a girl's body, greets us outside. He's smoking a cigarette and he says, sarcastically, "It's getting pretty wild up there." He continues, less sarcastically, "Some girls might take their shirts off. I'm gonna bring some pot."

"What's the deal with someone being born into a girl's body but identifying as a boy but then attending an all-girls school?" I ask Emma as we make our way up the stairs. "Does Ryan become ineligible to attend an all-girls school? Not that he should . . ."

"I don't know." Emma shrugs. "He probably applied and got in when he was still a girl."

13

An hour later, at the all-girls party in a dimly lit dorm room on the top floor of one of the dorms at the all-girls school, me and eight girls sit on the floor around a hookah and smoke orange-flavored tobacco as rap plays softly out of a pair of computer speakers and a really tall girl takes pictures of everyone. The party is in full swing and it doesn't seem like any of these people will be taking their shirts off. Ryan lies on the bed on his back, looking up at the ceiling.

I think about how this is not like a party in New York and I wish Ian and Mike were here to meet some of these single girls who don't get to interact with men that much. Emma sits next to me and talks to her best friend, Kate, about one of their classes, and two of the girls are holding hands and all of the girls furtively look at me. I guess, like Emma suggested, they're unaccustomed to being around men, especially in their space. The tall girl taking pictures fidgets nervously. I wonder if every person at this college gets their period at the same time. The person who works the convenience store on the way from the train station to the dorm building must know if there's a synchronized tampon rush every month, but I don't think I could bring myself to ask. A girl brings in an eighteen-pack of Coors Light and hands some of them out and then hands me one.

I stand up and look out the window of the dorm room at the

parking lot below, which is mostly empty, and then I come and sit back down again. A very thin and meek girl in sweatpants sitting to my left taps me on the shoulder. "So what kind of music do you listen to?"

This is a really hard question to answer. "Mostly Belle and Sebastian, I guess."

"Do you listen to any rap?"

"Yeah, I listen to some rap. Lil Wayne." She nods and looks down, waiting for me to reciprocate the question, and I look at the speakers and ask, "Did you put this playlist on? I like it." She smiles and nods and says, "It's actually an album, not a playlist. It's good, right?" I nod and she says, "It got reviewed on Pitchfork today and it only got a 6.1. I hate that website."

I say, "Me too! I think it's the thing I hate most on earth. Maybe it's the only thing I hate?"

"What's Pitchfork?" Emma asks.

I say, "It's a music reviews website. It's kind of the only one that matters — it has a huge readership and their reviews basically make or break bands."

The girl next to me chimes in, "The founder was on *Time* magazine's 100 Most Influential People list."

I continue, "Anyone who listens to indie music has an opinion about Pitchfork. I just hate it and wish it would go away. The writing is really bad a lot of the time, but nobody reads beyond the 0-to-10 score that they give each album, and it just seems insane to rate art on a numerical scale."

14

We go on for another few minutes and then run out of things to say about Pitchfork, and then I turn around and Emma is gone and has been replaced by a small girl wearing cutoff jean shorts. "Are you David?" she asks coldly.

I nod and she says, "Emma told me about you. I'm Erica." We shake hands and she asks, "So what do you do?" I tell her I just got a job working at the Fire Department Pension Fund and she says, "What kind of job?" I think for a second and say, "I do projections and estimates on firefighters' pensions and pension loans."

This sounds plausible and I am proud of myself for generating such a plausible lie on the spot.

"Wait. You went to NYU, right? And you're working at the fire department? Did you study philosophy or something?"

"Yeah, it turns out the philosophy companies aren't hiring right now" — even though I didn't study philosophy. Erica tells me that she has a job as a copyeditor at the *Atlantic* lined up when she graduates. I look around to see if I can escape or if Emma can extricate me from this, and I think about the *Seinfeld* episode where Jerry and Elaine are at a party in Long Island and they set up a system of physical signals to extricate each other from painful conversations. I wish me and Emma had set something like that up but maybe someday we will.

I ask Erica if she'll excuse me because I have to "go to the head," which I heard on the Travel Channel means the bathroom of a ship and sounds more adult than "go to the bathroom" or "go pee," and she says, "There are no men's bathrooms here. You're either gonna have to pee outside or look like a pervert using the women's bathroom. Sorry if you have to take a shit."

I excuse myself and run into Emma in the hallway and ask if we can hang out near Ryan and smoke some pot with him because Erica is terrifying, and Emma says, "Sure! I told you she was, didn't I?"

"Well, yeah," I say, "but knowing in advance didn't really mitigate it."

Two hours later we walk back to Emma's dorm under a full moon and she smokes a cigarette. It's very quiet on the quad. I ask, "Is that what parties are typically like here?" She says, "Yeah. Was it lame? I know it's not like parties in New York, obviously," and I tell her, "The party was nice," even though I secretly wanted to leave the whole time.

She says, "I know it's lame. This school sucks and I can't wait to leave — I wish I'd gone to school in New York with you and Camilla." I tell her New York is really stressful and expensive and there are many things to not like about it and she kisses me on the ear, and then we get back to her room and have sex. She falls asleep in my arms before I have a chance to pee, so I just hold it in until the morning.

15

On Monday, my first day of work, I get up at 6:30 and shower and put on a pair of skinny slacks that fit me better when I bought them. I look at myself in the mirror and wish I had a more conservative haircut and more conservative glasses, smaller ones that look like the ones the guy's wearing on the poster for *A Serious Man*, for my first day at a seemingly serious institution. Mike fell asleep on the couch and is still lying there, so I try not to disturb him as I walk out the door. I take the subway down to City Hall and walk to my new office building, which looks older and like a sadder place to work than all the buildings around it. I get there fifteen minutes early and look for a good place to eat lunch, but then I wonder if I'll even have a lunch hour. Probably not, because I only work five hours a day. I text Emma, "Thanks again for letting me visit this weekend, I had a nice time." I look at newspapers and magazines on a magazine rack and take note of the fruit-and-vegetable cart that's on the corner.

I walk into the office building at 9:26 and take my backpack off and put it on an X-ray conveyor belt and walk through a metal detector. When I get through the metal detector without beeping, I wait for my bag to come through the other side of the X-ray conveyor belt machine, but it doesn't, because the conveyor belt isn't moving, because the two security guards who are looking at the screens on the other side of the conveyor belt are studying my backpack. They look at me suspiciously and then back to the screen, and one points to something on the screen. Another security guard stands off to the side, reading the *Daily News*, and I try to think of anything suspicious I might have in my bag but I can't, and then the bag comes out the other side and one security guard says, "Can you empty your bag please?" I say, "Okay, but it's my first day of work and I only have four minutes to make it in on time and there's nothing suspicious in my bag — could we do this later? Like when I leave? I promise I'll come back."

She shakes her head and says, "You shoulda got here fifteen minutes ago," and makes me take everything out of my bag and lay it out in front of her, including my iPod and headphones and splitter, some bottles of vitamins, an old *New York* magazine, a pack of Trident White, a spare laptop charger that I forgot was in there, some coins, some lint and scraps of paper that have built up at the bottom of the bag, and two pairs of 3D glasses that I always keep with me in case I'm movie-hopping and one of the movies happens to be in 3D so I don't have to buy a 3D ticket because those are more expensive. She picks up the laptop charger and looks it over with the other security guard, and I tell her, "That's just a laptop charger, I promise." They both look it over slowly and then hand it back to me. The second security guard nods at me and indicates that I can pass.

I take the elevator to the eighth floor and walk down a dreary linoleum hall with a popcorn ceiling and into Room 800 and ask the receptionist for Mr. Mangino, the director of Human Resources, and then sit down in one of the chairs near the receptionist's desk. My shirt comes untucked in the back when I sit down, so I surreptitiously jam it back into the pants. I look around the office and it seems oppressively municipal — gray in-dustrial carpeting, a maze of cubicles with brown dividers, gray filing cabinets with rust around the edges, fluorescent lights, gray ceiling fans with blades covered in dust. Those will prob-ably be turned on in the summer. The walls and ceilings are yel-lowing. There are windows, but they're difficult to see through because of the dust and scratches and stuff. It doesn't look like anything has changed or been cleaned since 1975.

I take out my BlackBerry and see that it's 9:31 and that Emma has texted me back, "I had a nice time too. I'll see you in New York soon," and I put my BlackBerry away because that text doesn't really demand a reply and I don't want to seem desperate or annoyingly chatty. I fold my hands in my lap and wait.

Mr. Mangino, the man I was interviewed by on the phone, comes around the receptionist's desk and asks me if I'm David and I say I am and it's nice to meet him, and we shake hands and then I stand up. He has slicked-back hair and a gruff voice and a Staten Island accent and looks like he might have been a fire-fighter about twenty years ago, and he says, "How was it gettin' down here? Any problems?" I tell him the trip was easy because I live in the East Village and then instantly realize I shouldn't have told him that because he already knows I went to a private college and now he knows I live in a pretty expensive neighbor-hood and haven't had a job after college (or in college, from my résumé) so he can deduce that I'm extensively supported by my parents, and it seems like people don't really like people who go to expensive colleges and live in expensive neighborhoods while still being supported by their parents after college.

He says, "Oh yeah, the Village? How do you like it up there?" I nervously correct him, because "the Village," meaning Green-wich Village or the West Village, is more expensive than the

East Village and I don't want him to think I'm living in an even more expensive place. I say, nervously, because it's hard to not correct people even when I know I shouldn't, "Well, it's the East Village, not exactly the Village. 'The Village' refers to only Greenwich Village, I think, or I guess anywhere between Houston Street and 14th Street that's west of Fourth Avenue . . ." and he thinks about that for a second and says, "It's still the Village, just the east part of it. Right? It's called the East Village, not *east of the Village*. That's Alphabet City." He smiles because he knows I won't argue again so he has won, and I shrug and nod because I can't really think of how to continue this line of conversation in a way that would be profitable for me, and he also might be right.

But then we're at a conversational impasse and we stand there for a second looking at each other. I think of something to say, which is, "So, yeah, I sort of like living there. I live with four roommates" — a lie — "in a room that's so small that I can stand on my bed with my arms outstretched and touch the walls on opposite sides of the room" — also a lie. "I use the side of my bed as my chair at my desk, and two sides of the bed touch the opposite walls. It's a queen-size bed but still, you know, a tiny room."

He seems to find the reported size of my room novel. He says, "Sounds like city real estate. Out on Staten Island, you know, you get a good price. Still cheap out there." He doesn't really seem like a guy who'd be working in Human Resources, but maybe he was a firefighter and got injured and got put on desk duty as the director of Human Resources.

I nod and roll with the fact that he seems to be getting a kick out of how small my room is and tell him a story I heard at a party, substituting myself for the storyteller: "One time, one of my roommate's sisters came to visit New York from Florida, and she and her boyfriend took turns taking pictures of each other with their arms outstretched and touching the opposite walls, standing on my bed, because they thought it was a really funny New Yorky thing that a bedroom could be so small." He smiles at my relative misfortune and I am glad we can bond over it.

He asks, "You want a tour of the office? Or you want me to just show you to your desk?"

I say, "I think I'd like the tour, if that's okay with you, and then we could stop at my desk last?" He grins and asks, "You not eager to get to work?"

We walk past rows of cubicles in the Retirement Counseling section, where some middle-aged women are meeting with firefighters and discussing their pensions, I guess. One of the counselors swivels her computer monitor around to face the firefighter so she can show him a spreadsheet. Behind another one of the counselors, an ancient air conditioner is haphazardly jammed into a window with what looks like a towel and some curtain rods. Mr. Mangino introduces me to a counselor, a woman in her fifties with a Caribbean accent and huge boobs, and she greets me with a big handshake and asks me what I'm doing, and Mr. Mangino says, "He's working in the file room." She asks if I'm in school and I tell her I graduated, and she asks me where I graduated from and I say NYU, and then she goes, incredulously and attempting a twisted sort of compliment about the kind of jobs my schooling might have qualified me for, "Why are you working *here?*" She turns to Mr. Mangino and says, "In the file room?" She turns back to me and says, "In the file room of all places!" I tell her, earnestly, that the job is a great opportunity for me and she laughs. The tour continues.

A woman who weighs at least four hundred pounds, wearing a muumuu and holding a cane, walks down a hallway near us. Mr. Mangino says, "That's Harriet." A bald man in the Accounting section works on a calculator with a paper ticker readout, and a man with a prosthetic arm operates a mouse, moving it very slowly across the mouse pad and lifting his whole arm up before lowering it to click the mouse. He looks up at me and Mr. Mangino and gives Mr. Mangino a quizzical look, and Mr. Mangino goes, "He's the new guy in the file room." I ask Mr. Mangino if I will be working with these specific people or if my job will be limited to the file room, and he says I might work with them, but I shouldn't worry about trying to remember their names now, "if that's what you're worried about."

I lose focus on the tour and accidentally start to wonder whether I've made it through twenty-one years of life without ever having formed a genuine connection with another person, and if conversation is so difficult for everyone, and if there might be a medication I could take, that would actually work, that would make it easier to interact with people.

We pass a huge mural painting of firefighters standing together in front of the rubble of the Twin Towers. The words "Never Forget" are above them. There are framed photographs and paintings of firefighters on the walls, which date back to the late 1800s, and many of the cubicle walls have newspaper clippings from the *Post* and the *Daily News* tacked up on them: some about 9/11, some about Barack Obama, some negative ones about Mayor Bloomberg. One of the cubicles in the Accounts Payable section has a whole page taken out of the *Daily News* dedicated to the Jets that says, "J-E-T-S JETS! JETS! JETS!" The fluorescent lights need to be replaced and have dead flies in them.

I ask Mr. Mangino if I will get a lunch hour and he says, with some amusement, "Dave, come on. You only work five hours a day. If you get hungry during that time, you could bring something in and eat it at your desk." He says it like he knows I'm trying to shave a few minutes off my workday, but also like he knows that I know that he knows that I'm trying to shave a few minutes off my workday, so it's frank and friendly.

Our tour arrives at the kitchenette area, including a refrigerator and a sink and a water cooler and some baking trays full of plastic cutlery, and he tells me that the refrigerator gets cleaned on the last day of every month so I shouldn't leave food in there on the last day of the month, and also I need to label my food.

I say, "What if the last day of the month falls on a weekend and nobody is in the office — does the refrigerator get cleaned on the Friday or the Monday?"

"What does it matter?"

I say, "Well, if it gets cleaned on the Monday, then I'll know I have the option of coming in very early on the Monday morning to save the food."

He sighs again and says, "Just put a label on the food and you won't have to worry about it."

Then we walk into the file room, which has two desks next to each other, and Mr. Mangino introduces me to the occupants of those desks: "Tommy, the file room assistant" and "Dolores, the file room director." Tommy is pudgy and white and looks about thirty. He has a chin strap and is wearing a baggy Sean John polo shirt and baggy khakis and Nike ACG boots, and Dolores looks Hispanic and is about four foot nine and tremendously fat for her height and has a surgical scar under her neck. Her face is cherubic. I ask Mr. Mangino if my title is also file room assistant and he says, "No, you're the file room *associate.*

I'm gonna leave you here, and I'll be back later to bring you your paperwork." He walks out.

Dolores leads me through an endless field of filing cabinets that are filled, floor to ceiling, with manila folders full of fire-fighters' pension files. My desk is all the way at the back of the file room, in an area with no windows and no computer, next to a microfiche machine and some typewriters that look like they fell out of use when the office started using computers proba-bly about fifteen years ago. In a fortress of municipal decrepi-tude, I might be in the dungeon of decrepitude, unless there's a worse area to be in that I haven't seen yet. I ask, "I don't get a computer?" She says, without affectation, "You don't need a computer. Nothing you do is on the computer." We look at each other, and I think about how she and Tommy have computers. I think this is a hierarchical thing.

We walk back to Dolores's desk and she says, matter-of-factly, "Who was your hook?" I ask, "What do you mean by 'hook'?" She looks at me and says, "Who got you this job? No-body here gets jobs without hooks. So who was your hook?"

I say, "I . . . Well . . . I guess it was Linda Greenberg," and she looks me up and down with distaste and nods. Dolores doesn't seem to like Linda Greenberg, and I want to tell her that I don't like Linda Greenberg either because whenever Linda Green-berg sees me she asks me what my plans are for my future, the question I hate most, and she also may have just gotten me this job to show off to my mom or so my mom might owe her a fa-vor, but it doesn't seem like the right time to tell this to Dolores because she might have a greater allegiance to Linda Greenberg than to me and tell her.

Dolores explains the dual responsibilities of my job, which

include filing stacks of papers and pulling folders out of the filing cabinets upon request. Before I file, I will receive a stack of papers labeled with the firefighters' ID numbers on them, and then I have to go through the filing cabinets, match the ID number on the piece of paper to the ID number on the firefighter's folder, and put the piece of paper into the folder. Before I pull folders, I will receive a list of firefighters' ID numbers whose folders need to be pulled; then I will go through the filing cabinets and pull the folders and put them on a little cart thing, and then wheel the cart over to the front of the file room, where it will be picked up by the person who requested it. Some days, there is little work or no work and I can read a book or a magazine.

As we come back to Dolores's desk, Tommy is walking into the hallway, so he's out of earshot. "What does Tommy do?" I ask.

"Here's how the whole thing works: The files come in. I put them into the computer. Tommy carries the files over to your desk. You file them." I ask why Tommy and I have different job titles, and she says, "Because he's older. He's been here longer. He's more senior."

16

By noon, I've filed hundreds of pieces of paper and pulled about a hundred folders and I'm sitting at my desk again because there's no more filing work. I get up to go to the bathroom, and Tommy and Dolores sit at their desks and stare blankly at their computer screens, like people on airplanes who bring nothing to read or to listen to during the flight, like David Puddy on *Seinfeld*. I don't know if they're connected to the Internet. I walk down the hallway, past the break room, where *Family Feud* is on TV and some of my coworkers eat fast-food lunches and scream the answers along with the contestants, like in a mental asylum. This is New York City's municipal middle class, I think: people who make five times as much money working for the government as they could working for a private company and who are impossible to fire. Now I am one of them, sort of. When I come back to my desk, I read the day's Pitchfork reviews on my BlackBerry at my desk and get mad about two of them, send Mike an email about how outrageous one of the scores is and why it is outrageous, and stare at the wall. Mr. Mangino comes by to bring me the paperwork I have to fill out, and I fill it out and bring it back to him and go back to my desk as the newest member of the clerical workers' union.

17

March and April pass with me mostly among stacks of files and, some weekends, in Emma's dorm room. Mike gets a freelance blogging/reporting job, so he blogs from our couch and makes almost enough money to not need his parents to help with his rent and cell phone bill. He writes about celebrities for a celebrity blog aimed at educated people. Sometimes he gets to go to galas and benefits to interview celebrities about their careers and current events that are either straightforwardly relevant to the celebrity or comically juxtaposed with the public perception of that celebrity. I'm jealous of his job because it seems glamorous and more engaging than my job, but sometimes he lets me come with him to celebrity parties to eat free hors d'oeuvres, drink free liquor, and lurk near where famous people are eating. I only have two outfits that are nice enough to wear to parties like these, so when they both get food and wine stains on them, I have to take them to the Laundromat and don't get to go to that night's party.

Ian, who graduated NYU magna cum laude with a degree in economic policy, also in three and a half years like me, gets a job as a cater waiter for a catering company based in Midtown and makes enough money to support himself without the help of his parents and without going into debt, an immense accomplishment. He seems happy with his situation because he can choose exactly how much he wants to work and therefore how much money he wants to make, which he points out is not an option afforded by conventional jobs.

He also writes unpaid blog posts for a blog about microfinance in Bangladesh and uses the extra money he makes from catering to buy textbooks about microfinance, and then sometimes we get drunk and he tells me about how the microfinance system is broken but it's the best chance poor people around the world have to extricate themselves from poverty, and then he gets drunkenly sentimental and we look at pictures of starving children on slideshows on South Asian newspapers' websites.

One night in April, Mike is covering the same gala that Ian is catering and so the three of us take the subway up there together. On the subway, Mike tells us some of the questions that he's thinking about asking the celebrities at the gala, and we go back and forth trying to decide if they're funny or not funny. When we get to the hotel that the gala is at, Ian goes inside and me and Mike go into the Apple Store on 59th Street to do some last-minute research on the celebrities.

An hour later, we get to the gala and Bill Clinton is there, and Mike elicits a funny quote from him about how many babies he estimates he has kissed and hands he estimates he's shaken over the course of his political career. I stand in the corner of the room taking pigs in blankets off an unattended tray and hoping nobody notices me. An attractive woman with visible cleavage looks at me and I instinctively look down.

Then, as Bill Clinton is leaving the gala a few hours later, he walks through the kitchen and thanks each member of the catering staff individually, including Ian, who at the time has his hands covered in some sticky food. Bill Clinton shakes Ian's sticky hand and doesn't even flinch or stop smiling, and later Ian tells me, "That guy's a fucking pro."

Me and Emma text each other every day, but sometimes we can't go back and forth for that long because she's working on her thesis, which is broadly in biology but it's hard to know specifically because she never wants to talk about it. Sometimes when she comes to New York she has to spend alone time with Camilla because the afternoon after me and Emma first hooked up and she went back to school, Camilla sent her an email saying that if we started hooking up after she set us up and stopped hanging out with her when we were both in town, she would "not like either of you very much anymore!!!!"

18

One night at the end of January, me and Emma are lying in her bed, listening to jj. Emma touches my hand and takes a breath and says, as if she is revealing something really major: "I feel like I've known you for a very long time."

"You have. Remember that party on your roof like two years ago?"

She says, "No, I didn't mean like that. Like I feel like I've known you, like, for a lot of my life. Even if we hadn't met yet. Does that make sense?"

"Sort of. Not really. I'm, ummmm . . . I'm very literal. You've known me for a little less than two years." I think I know what she means, but it's not easy for me to talk about major romantic things like this, or really any romantic things, and I know Emma will understand, so I don't amend my response.

She pulls the covers over our heads and squeezes my hand like she's trying to get me to understand what she's saying with the squeeze. I get up and grab my iPod and headphone splitter and two pairs of headphones and get back under the covers, and we both put the headphones on and listen to the original version of "Judy and the Dream of Horses" from *If You're Feeling Sinister*, and then the rerecorded version of it from *If You're Feeling Sinister: Live at the Barbican*. They rerecorded *If You're Feeling Sinister* because they didn't like how the original sounded.

And after we finish listening to both recordings of the song, she says that when she had only heard the first one, she thought, "Why would they rerecord this song? It's already perfect," but now, after she has heard the rerecorded version, she says she thinks, "It's slightly more perfect."

Then I think about what I'm going to say for a second and say, "I agree with what you're saying, but I think not with the way you're saying it. Something can't be more perfect than something else that is also perfect."

She says, "Why not?"

And I say it's because perfection is an absolute state and there can't be something that's more in an absolute state than something else in the same absolute state. Something can't be "a little perfect" or "totally perfect," it can just be either perfect or not perfect, and two perfect things can't be more or less perfect than each other.

I say, "It's like that *Seinfeld* episode where the characters talk about whether there are degrees of coincidence, like small coincidences or big coincidences, or whether all coincidences are equal. I'm not sure which one of those is right, but I'm pretty positive that one thing can't be more perfect than any other perfect thing."

She looks around the room for a while, taking in the dorm chair and the little desk and the light shining through the window from the streetlamps in the quad, and says, "Times like these are when the appeal of who you are simultaneously really shines through and becomes really unclear to me. Do you know what I mean?"

I say, "Sort of?" and she says, "It's because you seem to have a hard time discerning anybody else's mental state, which is annoying because it's easier to deal with empathetic people, but also liberating because I don't become emotionally dependent on your intuitive reassurances, like I would if I was dating someone from this planet."

I smile and say, "I am from this planet," and then she rolls over and is about to get out of bed and asks, "Do you want a snack?"

"I don't think so. Couples eating snacks in bed is like the second fattest thing on earth, after this pair of sweatpants that I used to have when I was obese. The sweatpants were dyed and stitched to look like jeans, and some kid in my ninth-grade art class who was also really fat looked at me and pointed to my sweatpants and said, 'Sweatpants made to look like jeans are the fattest thing on earth.'"

She gets back in bed and hugs me and says, "I've definitely seen animals and people that are fatter than sweatpants made to look like jeans."

19

On an afternoon in the middle of May, Emma sounds weird on the phone and I ask her if everything is okay and she says, "Yeah, everything is fine," in the tone where you know everything is not fine but there's no reason to press it because the person who's not fine isn't going to reveal why in this conversation.

I take the Chinatown bus and then the commuter rail out to her school, and she picks me up at the train station but waits in the car instead of coming out to the platform to get me. I get into the car and NPR is playing softly, and Emma kisses me but doesn't look me in the eye. She starts the car and we drive away from the train station and down the main road in the college's town, and we talk about how her brassicas are growing.

We pull into the parking lot of the convenience store near her college. We get out of the car and go into the store, and she picks up a bag of honey-wheat pretzel rods and I grab some Coors Lights out of the fridge, and then we get up to the counter and she asks for a pack of Camel Lights and pays, and then I sheepishly ask for condoms and then pay for the beer and the condoms. When we step outside, I say, "I can tell that something is wrong, Emma — what's wrong?"

She says, "Nothing. I don't want to talk about it now. Let's get back in the car. It's freezing, honey." She shivers a little and breathes and looks at her breath in the air to prove how cold it is.

We get into the car, and she starts the car and breathes hot air into her hands and rubs them together and looks upset, and I say, "Okay, something is clearly wrong. What is it?"

We drive for about thirty seconds in silence before she says anything. Then she looks at me and says, sullenly, "I got a temporary job for after graduation," and then she looks back at the road.

I look excitedly at her and go, "Ah, that's great. That's amazing. What kind of job?"

She says, "Working and coordinating work on a farm."

I think for a second and say, "So then what's the problem? Why are you upset?"

We drive for another ten seconds and then she looks at me and says, "It's for seven months . . . and it's in California."

"So we wouldn't be able to see each other?"

She says, hesitantly, "You could come visit me," and I say, "I don't think I have the money for that," and she says, "Could you ask your parents for the money?"

I consider that for a second and realize it's not feasible because they'd never give me money to fly all the way across the country to visit a non-Jewish girl, and then I say, "I don't think they'd give me it," and she says, "Why?" and I say, "They said they've given me enough money already and to stop asking."

Emma looks disappointed. I ask, "Are you sure you're definitely going? Are there no other jobs you could find?"

She says, "Yeah, I have to go. I didn't get any other offers after sending out a million résumés, and this one happens to pay pretty well." We'd talked about having trouble finding jobs before, but I didn't know she'd been applying across the country. It wasn't nice that she didn't tell me, but pointing that out wouldn't accomplish anything.

I don't know what to say so I ask, "What kind of farm is it?"

"A huge farm in Marin County, just north of San Francisco, and it's in a beautiful valley, and they have plenty of livestock and flowers and gardens, and they grow all sorts of crops, including both brassicas and probably weed, though it didn't say weed on the website, but it just has that sort of vibe."

"We should go on Google Maps Street View and see if we can see any wild weed growing on the mountainsides from the road."

"It's so idyllic — if there is a way that you could come visit me there, I'd squeeze my hand so hard your fingers would break." We pull into the parking lot in her dorm and she turns the car off, and we get out of the car and close the doors behind us and come around the back of the car, and I put my arms around her and we kiss for a second, and then she lays her head against my chest for about five minutes and maybe sobs softly. I think I can sort of feel it through the hood of her jacket, but I might be imagining it, but given the circumstances it seems likely. I don't think I will visit her; I don't want to see the men she works around and have to wonder if she's sleeping with them.

20

On a Sunday morning two weekends later, me and Emma sleep in Shira's room in Camilla's apartment again because Shira is out of town again. I wake up first and I look at Emma, and then she wakes up and looks at me and yells, almost at the top of her lungs, "Stop looking at me, swan!" like from *Billy Madison*. She smiles at me and breathes morning breath into my face.

I come out into the living room, and Camilla is sitting on the couch, watching TV and trying to do her homework. She looks up at me and says, "Stop looking at me, swan. I'm trying to do my homework, swan."

"Why are you calling me 'swan'?" She says, "Isn't that what Emma calls you?" I say, "She was quoting *Billy Madison*. It's not an all-the-time thing." I walk over and sit down next to Camilla. I ask if she has seen *Billy Madison*, and she says, "Yeah," and I say, "You don't remember that line though? That was one of the most key lines in the film," and she says, "It just slipped my mind." She looks down at her homework again and crosses something out harshly with her pen.

"Is everything okay with you?" I ask, and Camilla says, "No, everything is not okay with me. Where is your roommate? He's not picking up my calls or answering my texts. Why is it okay to date me for a year and then dump me and then fuck me whenever he feels like it and then not pick up my calls or answer my texts? I don't understand. Where is he?"

Mike slept over at this girl Angelica's house last night, I think, so I say, "No idea? Maybe he's at home with his parents or maybe his phone broke. Or, like, you know he always loses it and stuff. Just give him a minute."

"You know that's not true. You know where he is, you're just not telling me."

"Hey, just relax and let's go get brunch, and then I'm sure by the time we're done he will have called or texted you back." Camilla agrees to go to brunch, and so I go back into Shira's room and put on my hoodie and pick up my BlackBerry and text Mike: "Hey man, call Camilla back and make something up about last night, I just covered for you and she seems mad."

Me and Emma and Camilla walk to a diner on Houston Street, and on our way there Mike texts me back, "Okay I'll call her back now." Then Camilla gets a call from Mike and she walks out of earshot and they talk for about five minutes.

"Mike's coming to meet us for brunch."

I say, unthinkingly, "Are you mad at him?"

She looks at me suspiciously and says, "Why would I be mad at him? He just woke up. His phone died while he was sleeping . . . Is there something I should be mad about?" I shake my head and turn back to Emma.

21

Half an hour later in the diner, I am complaining about Pitchfork to Mike. Camilla and Emma are talking about meeting up with one of the other girls they went to boarding school with, and we are all eating different kinds of omelets.

Emma and Camilla's conversation sort of drops off and they start listening to ours. I'm in the middle of saying, "Stewart Morrison is a buffoon. I think he's the worst staff writer they've ever had."

Mike says, "Why? I think he's average."

"His writing is like knee-jerk message-board style. You remember when the guy from Bon Iver went on like a two-hour Twitter rant about him?"

Emma says, with affection and exasperation, "Honey, could you stop complaining about this all the time and do something about it?"

I say, "The problem is that there's nothing you can do about it because the site doesn't have a comments section so there's no way for listeners to make their opinions known to the writers. You can't even email them because their email addresses aren't public! That's why I get like this." Mike and Camilla laugh but I'm not joking, but I understand why they're laughing.

Camilla takes a bite of her omelet and Emma says, "Why don't you start a blog where you write reviews of their reviews?

That's what I would do if I were you. You could just write every-thing that you want to write about each of their reviews and get it out of your system, and then maybe other Internet mu-sic herbs like you would be really into it." Camilla giggles at the word "herbs," pronounced with a strong *H* sound.

Mike asks me to pass the ketchup so I pass it, and then as he's pouring it I say, "Do you wanna hear a cool fact about ketchup?" Mike nods and I go, "It's the world's only perfect food. There are five flavors that food can have: bitter, sour, salty, sweet, and umami." Mike gives me a quizzical look so I continue, "Umami is, like, savory. And ketchup is the only food in the world that has all five flavors. Isn't that cool?" Mike and Camilla and Emma nod, and I look at Emma and say, "I mean, it's perfect in one way, like obviously you wouldn't want to eat only ketchup, but it makes sense in this particular scheme." Emma smiles like she's remembering the last time we talked about perfect things but doesn't say anything.

22

We pay the check and start walking back to Camilla's house. I ask Mike, "Do you think people would read a website of reviews of Pitchfork reviews? There are a lot of random people out there who hate Pitchfork." Mike shrugs and says, "I would read yours. But maybe only because I know you. I guess it depends on if it's good or interesting or not, you know?" I nod and look around to see if Camilla and Emma are within earshot, and then I lower my voice and say, "How was last night?" Mike says, quietly, "It was okay. She was kind of boring. She didn't really say that much. She wasn't cute enough to be as boring as she was, but not so overwhelmingly boring or uncute that it was a deal-breaker. I had to do most of the talking. But I had a good time." I ask, "What'd you do?" He looks behind us at Emma and Camilla, who are about half a block back.

"We took a walk around downtown Manhattan and then we wanted to drink, so we went into the W Hotel that's by Ground Zero and took the elevator up into their lounge on the fifth floor. There was a bar and a DJ and a lot of the hotel patrons were dancing. Like, Midwestern tourists. So we just drank and watched people dance and then made out on this couch by the window overlooking Ground Zero. Then we went out to the balcony and looked at Ground Zero and made out for like another ten minutes."

"Like the episode where Jerry goes on a date to the movies and gets caught making out with his date during *Schindler's List!*" Mike nods and then sees Camilla and Emma coming up next to us, and his eyes widen in near panic and he looks at me, thinking about if he is caught. "What's like that episode?" Camilla says. I say, hoping it comes out playfully, "I was just telling Mike some private stuff, please butt out," and she looks at me suspiciously and says, "First of all, 'butt out' sounds like something a fifty-seven-year-old woman would say. Second of all, what stuff?"

"Man stuff," and then she says, "Neither of you are men," and I say, "Okay, fine, boy stuff."

23

We get back to Camilla's apartment, and Mike and Emma and Camilla sit down on the couch, and Camilla turns on the TV and changes the channel to Bravo, and I sit down at the living room table, facing the TV so I can look at the TV and the Internet at the same time. There is a reality dating show on and I think, "The people on this show look like idiots," which I realize is good because it means I am feeling riled up right now, which puts me in the right frame of mind to write about Pitchfork. I ask Mike what the current cool blogging platform is.

I say, "If I'm going to start a blog, I don't want to do it on an outdated platform like WordPress or Blogspot that people would dismiss before reading it . . ." Mike thinks for a second and says, "You should start a Tumblr, it's the cool one right now."

So I go on Tumblr and register a blog called Pitchfork Reviews Reviews, and then I bring the laptop over to Mike, who logs into his Tumblr account and becomes my first follower. Camilla says, "You're actually doing this?" and I nod.

"Have you ever written anything before?"

I say, "Papers in college and high school." I bring the laptop back to the table and start writing a screed against Pitchfork, which is titled "Pitchfork Reviews Reviews Rationale" and includes several of the points I discussed with the girl at that party at Emma's college and some other points, as well as some lines in all caps and a lot of exclamation points.

It feels good to organize all of the things I have been thinking and also feel like I am throwing a tiny stone across the Internet at the walls of the fortress of Pitchfork's unfortunate cultural tyranny, or something. After I finish the entry, I sign it "anonymous because potential employers will be Googling me." I say to Mike, "Hey, so I don't have a computer at work — could I send you the entries from my BlackBerry and you'd post them on my Tumblr? Otherwise I would have to wait until I get home to post them, and I'd rather have them up early, and also you're at the computer all day . . ." Mike says, "Sure. You're really doing this?" and I say, "Definitely. Also, could you also not tell anyone that I write it on my BlackBerry and email it to you? I don't think people would take it seriously if they found out it was written by a guy on his BlackBerry."

"Okay," Mike says.

I imagine Pitchfork writers getting miffed about this if they ever saw it, and maybe being forced to think about the kind of destruction they're causing to bands who are just starting to develop but are thrust into the spotlight prematurely by a good Pitchfork review with a really high score before they've even played like ten shows and they have no business being scrutinized like fully formed bands yet. I think about how many bands Pitchfork has destroyed for one reason or another, but I know that it's impossible to calculate. I hope Pitchfork writers are troubled by what I have to say, and that they think about all of the smaller music websites that have folded because Pitchfork has dominated them and usurped all their traffic, even though it's not good that there is just one significant voice in online alternative music criticism now, but of course it's unlikely that any Pitchfork writers will ever read what I've written, but maybe someday one of them could come across it.

For a second, I wonder if I just use Pitchfork as a lightning rod for how disappointed I feel about almost everything in my life, but that's beside the point. I imagine Pitchfork writers, tall men who have figured out how to make livings thinking and writing about music, drinking Hoegaardens on the rooftops of their Brooklyn luxury condos, watching the sunset with hot girls wearing American Apparel and no bras, each one of them sometimes considering how they personally have the power to shift the landscape of independent music every time they pick a CD up out of the pile of promos that record labels send them. I imagine them trading clever messages on a private message board about which bands' careers they're going to end for no reason, and which fly-by-night bands they're going to trick people into listening to by giving their records glowing reviews even though the writers themselves know they're shitty. I can see them hanging out with indie starlets like Greta Gerwig at loft parties, walking outside to smoke with them, and then running into people who work at magazines who are also smoking outside and all of them talking and laughing together.

Pitchfork's logo is three arrows pointing to the northeast, so I use a program on Camilla's laptop to flip that logo so it's pointing to the southwest, and then I make that my logo and upload it to Tumblr so it appears on the top of my blog. I say to everyone in the room, "That's clever, right? Right?" Emma thinks about this for a second and nods.

After I post the entry, I think about it for a second and feel pretty satisfied with it and hand the laptop back to Mike, and he clicks the Like button on the entry and then he reblogs the entry. Mike has about three hundred followers, most of whom work for Internet media outlets in New York, so I hope some of them will see the link and then click on the link to my blog and become my followers too.

24

Later that night, I walk Emma back to the subway again because she has to go back to school. She asks if I will come visit her next weekend and I say I will, and then we kiss and then she gets on the subway. I walk home and think about how many readers I'd like to have ideally, which is probably around three hundred like Mike's Tumblr, but it will take me a long time to get there. When I get home, Mike is using the Internet on the couch. "So is Emma your girlfriend?" he says. I say, "Why do you always ask me?" Mike says, "I'm just curious," and I shake my head and say, "I don't think so? We don't talk about it. I think it's better that way." Then I go into my room and check my Tumblr, and I already have fifteen followers just off that one entry, including a user from Germany who left a comment that says, "Totally agree 100%."

25

The next morning I wake up and roll over and grab my Black-Berry off my nightstand and go onto Pitchfork and read the beginning of the first review and think of things to say about it. Then I look at the clock, and I should already have been in the shower by now, so I go take a shower and get dressed and then leave my building and walk to the subway and read the rest of the first Pitchfork review as I walk. I won't be able to read the second, third, fourth, and fifth reviews on the subway because I won't have cell phone service in the subway, so I load the fifth review, then the fourth, then the third, then the second, then the first. On the subway I finish reading the first review and write a paragraph about it in an email to Mike in the Gmail client on my BlackBerry. Then I click the back button and read the second review and write a paragraph about it. Then I get to work.

I walk through the file room, past Tommy and Dolores. Tommy is staring blankly at his computer screen again, and Dolores is reading the *New York Post* online. I can't see what the story is, but I can see the *Post*'s logo, and I suspect it's the crime blotter. One time when I was filing, I overheard her say, "Crime's really getting bad," and Tommy said, "Oh yeah, it's gettin' bad everywhere."

There's a big stack of papers on my desk and I file them as fast as I can and then get back to reading the rest of the reviews and writing about them. After I have written about four of the reviews, Tommy comes into my area at the back of the file room and stands there for a second and looks at me typing on my phone. He says, "What're you doing?" I tell him I'm writing an email to my mom, and he asks what it's about, and I tell him it's about visiting home soon. He asks where my parents live and I say, "In the suburbs." Then he walks back to his desk, and when I'm done I proofread everything I've written and send it to Mike, who posts it on my Tumblr. I do this every day for the whole week and then by the end of the week I have fifty-five followers. It feels awesome that all these people have decided to subscribe to what I am writing. Most of them are between the ages of fourteen and seventeen, but I really feel like I am hitting my stride with what I am saying. Some days I write thousands of words and they just flow out, like from a river in my brain that I didn't even know was there before I started writing about Pitchfork.

I write two posts a day. In my post in the mornings I criticize the foundations of the reviews' arguments, agree with foundations of other reviews' arguments. I point out typos and predict which forthcoming records will be receiving high scores. I even start assigning my own scores to Pitchfork reviews. Occasionally I commend a review for making a really interesting point, but I try to counterbalance that with a really scathing review of a different review so my readers won't think I'm soft on Pitchfork.

In the afternoons I write my second post, which is a little snippet about my own relationship to the records I listen to or an important experience or realization I had while listening to a record. One day I write about listening to Bob Marley at summer camp with camp counselors; one day I write about how the fat white guy who plays guitar and is in Lil Wayne's crew is the last rock star on earth by a very narrow definition. Another day I write about playing the first Beirut album for my dad and Bubba because it sounds like Eastern European folk music, and how they reacted to it, and how I think about my dad. I feel accomplished when I get home from work.

26

Two weeks from the day I started I have 136 followers, and then the Monday after that I have 350 followers, and then the Monday after that I have 572 followers, and a small music site has linked to one of my entries and agreed with it, but also one of my followers has reblogged one of my entries and written "THIS GUY IS A MORON—UNFOLLOWED" above it, meaning that he thinks I'm a moron and that he has unfollowed my blog, which hurts and makes me wonder why he even followed it in the first place. When I read that, I sit at my desk at work and look at the yellowing walls and the unopened boxes of typewriter ribbons from fifteen years ago that are on the metal shelves around my desk and think, "Like, why am I even doing this?"

I call Emma and she is playing Frisbee on the quad at school with Ryan. I ask her if she has a minute to talk and she says, "Yeah, I do, what's up?" She can sense that something is wrong in my voice so she continues, "Is everything okay?"

"I don't know. One of my followers reblogged a post I wrote and called me a moron and said he was unfollowing me." Emma says, "Honeyyyyy, I'm sorryyyy, but you know you're great. You shouldn't worry about people like that. I read your posts and I think they're very good, and they look like they're getting more and more Notes."

I tell her, "Thanks, but it's just hard to keep the 'MORON' reblog out of my mind, you know?"

When I get home from work that day, I go onto the blog of the guy who wrote that I am a moron and find his email address and email him using my new email address, pitchforkreviews reviews@gmail.com, and say, "Hi, this is the Pitchfork Reviews Reviews Tumblr. I was wondering what your specific problem with my post was because you said something mean about it, and I know that at some point there was something you liked about my blog, enough to follow it, and then something that made you hate me all of a sudden, because I don't think I've been doing anything fundamentally different recently, and I was wondering what it was and if you would want to talk about it."

An hour later, an anonymous person from the Internet who I will never see or meet emails me back a long apology and tells me that he disagreed with my assessment of one aspect of one review, but it's hard to imagine that when you write mean things about people on the Internet, it might actually wind up hurting them in real life. He apologizes again and, two minutes later, re-follows my Tumblr.

27

The Monday after that, I have 765 followers and Mike texts me to express his happy surprise and congratulations. After I leave work, I decide to walk home and call my dad because I haven't called him in two weeks. I ask him what he's doing and he says, "I'm watching a YouTube, learning a lot about the Chinese. Did you know the Chinese government just bought a billion dollars worth of Mr. G?" "Mr. G" is what he calls gold on the phone in case the government has tapped his phone to keep tabs on his gold holdings for the imminent nationwide gold confiscation and law against gold ownership. Silver is "Mr. S." "And it shot up sixteen dollars in after-hours trading when they announced it."

"That's great! Sounds like you made a bunch of money to-day" — because he owns gold.

He says, "I wish I could tell you on the phone, but yes, a lot."

"So how's Mom?"

"Did you watch the YouTubes I emailed you?"

"No, I haven't had a chance to watch them yet."

"Why do you never listen? Why are you so resistant?" He sighs and continues, "Your father is trying to get you to understand the situation around the world and prepare you for the future, and you don't even click the YouTubes? Think, boy. As long as I am paying for you to live, at least you watch the You-Tubes. This is important. This is what Obama doesn't want you to see because he's trying to suffocate you under a mountain of debt!"

I picture him sitting in the basement in our house in front of his computer and two small TVs, one playing Fox News and one playing CNBC, and shaking his fist at Maria Bartiromo and screaming "NEVEILAH!," which loosely means "bitch" or something in Yiddish.

I ask again, "How's Mom?" I'm afraid this attempt to change the subject won't succeed either, but it does.

"She's fine. I think she's at the pool now, or in the garden. Are you doing your law school books?" He means studying for the LSAT.

"Yeah, every day."

"Good." Then he tries to think of something to say to me related to my personal life because maybe even he realizes that talking about gold and the rapidly collapsing global economy to the exclusion of everything else isn't the best way to maintain a relationship with his son. He says, "How is . . . How is . . . you know, the boy you live with? With the bikes?"

"He's good. He got a job blogging about celebrities." My dad processes that for a second and then curses under his breath in Russian.

"I hope you are not learning from him."

"No, I'm not." I am fifteen blocks from home and I say, "Okay, I'm just getting home now, so I'll talk to you soon."

"Remember to watch the YouTubes," he says, and hangs up.

28

When I get home, Mike is sitting on the couch.

"You wanna see something cool?" he says.

"Sure, what is it?"

He clicks on something and turns his computer screen toward me and shows me an email from someone at the website he works for, asking if he is secretly writing Pitchfork Reviews Reviews. He hasn't responded yet and we agree that he will respond no. I ask why the person would suspect a connection between us, and he says he thinks it's because he reblogged my first post like two minutes after I wrote it.

I go into my room and look at my LSAT prep book, still in its Amazon.com packaging, on my desk, and change out of my work clothes. I come back out into the living room and Mike says, "Good post today." I thank him, and then he says, "Do you wanna go to this blogger reading series tonight that my friend Lexi is putting on? We email sometimes and he follows your Tumblr and I think he'd want to meet you. He invited me and he said you should come too. His Tumblr name is Lexicrawl."

"Oh yeah," I say. "He reblogs some of my posts sometimes! Is it just, like, Internet writers reading their blog entries out loud?"

"Yeah, sort of, I think? I don't know, I've never been."

"Okay, that sounds like it might be okay."

Five hours later we walk to the West Village. Mike tells me

about seeing Angelica and Camilla at the same time and how it feels like juggling because it's hard to keep them from finding out about each other. I tell him I wish that my problem was too many women.

"That's not really what it is."

We keep walking and I say, "Have you ever met Lexi in person?"

"Yeah, once, at another one of these things."

"What does he do?"

"He writes about technology for the *New York Observer*."

"Did he go to NYU?"

Mike says, "No, Yale." I don't know anyone who went to Yale.

29

We get to the coffee shop where the reading is supposed to take place, and some kids standing around outside look very fashionable, like wearing rigid denim and shoes instead of sneakers. I look at my reflection in the window of a storefront a few doors down and comb my hair with my hand so it looks okay. We stand outside as Mike finishes his cigarette, and we can hear a girl behind us talking to a very tall guy about how Slate "spouts conventional wisdom disguised as innovative thinking — so dishonest." I want to turn around and tell her that there are plenty of worthwhile things on Slate that are just fun and good, like the Explainer column where the writer answers readers' questions that are related to the news, but we don't know each other, so it might be weird to go up to a random person and tell them you disagree with them, so I don't.

We go inside the coffee shop, and it is small and sort of quaintly decorated, with wooden floors and walls and black-and-white pictures hanging up all around. It is packed with about seventy-five well-dressed twenty- and thirty-somethings, many of whom are carrying tote bags from bookstores and magazines like *Harper's*, magazines that I've never read but that seem really impressive. I remind myself that coolness is just a characteristic people ascribe to people who they only observe from afar, and that nobody is actually cool once you get to know them, and especially not people who are really concerned about how they're dressed, but knowing that something is true and acting on it are different obviously.

There's a microphone set up at the front (and some chairs), and me and Mike squeeze through people until we get to the very back of the open space, as far from the microphone as possible. I take out my BlackBerry to text Emma something affectionate, but I have only a red sliver of battery life left, so I turn my BlackBerry off. Mike points to the tall guy who was talking outside. He says, "That's Lexi. We'll talk to him after it's over."

The bloggers start reading. A small girl with thick glasses reads a radical feminist take on a Weezer album, and then a guy who looks like he's in his thirties reads something satirical about his suburban Massachusetts mom and her friends who power walk and eat expensive kinds of cereal, and then a pretty girl reads about the things that she misses about New York when she is traveling. She's the one who was talking about Slate outside.

When the readings are finished, me and Mike walk outside and see Lexi in a circle of kids, including the Slate girl. She has a sharp face and laughs really loudly, like so loudly that when she laughs, people around her turn and look at her. People don't seem to mind. I guess this is the kind of trait that people would say was obnoxious if she wasn't a beautiful girl, but obviously beautiful girls can laugh however they want.

Lexi is smoking and Mike walks up near him and I walk behind Mike. When Lexi sees Mike, he turns to him and they greet each other with high fives that turn into handshakes and then start talking. I am standing behind Mike because I'm nervous to meet Lexi because he seems important and I don't want to make a bad impression on him.

Mike turns to me and introduces us, and I shake Lexi's hand weakly, and he looks down at me and smiles and says, "So you're the real Pitchfork Reviews Reviews kid! I love your stuff!" I say, "Thanks very much. I really liked your reading. It was great." The Slate girl taps Lexi on the shoulder and looks me and Mike over disinterestedly and says, "I think we're gonna start heading to the restaurant . . . ," and then Lexi turns back to us and says, "We're going to Spain, on 13th Street — do you guys wanna come?" Mike looks at me and I nod.

30

While we walk to the restaurant, Mike points out all the people he is familiar with that are walking with us to the restaurant, just so I know who they are when we get there and I don't have to ask anybody. Annie blogs for *Vanity Fair*, Michael works for Tumblr, Amanda started a funny blog about being a girl in her early twenties and currently has a book deal and a TV show concept in development based on it, Lexi writes for the *Observer* and went to Yale and is twenty-five, and Alexandra, the Slate girl, works at *Granta* and went to Harvard and is twenty-five too. Me and Mike are both twenty-one. Mike isn't familiar with three of the people we're walking with, but I am positive that none of these people are people who I want to tell that I work in the windowless armpit of the file room for the New York City Fire Department inside a crumbling city building, where I write a Tumblr from my BlackBerry, so I hope I can just ask them questions about their own careers until we can leave.

We get to Spain and the waiter seats us around a big table in the back of the restaurant and we order drinks. This is a cool restaurant. The waiters look like they're about a hundred years old, *Daily News* clippings from the '80s are posted outside, and the walls are lined with faded pictures of Spain (the country).

I get a Guinness because it is the lowest-calorie nonlight beer (almost no sugar) and I want to drink something low-

calorie but I don't want to get a light beer because then people will think I am concerned about calories. And also, people
think Guinness is really caloric because it feels heavy and frothy
and like a milk shake, so they think you're really not concerned
about calories and that you're a hedonist. I sit between Lexi and
Mike, and everyone talks about the reading, and they all seem
to know each other all pretty well, except me and Mike. A guy
in glasses across the table asks us who we know here. I point to
Lexi and stay silent and then Mike says, "Lexi." The guy across
the table says, "What do you guys do?"

Mike answers first and tells the guy across the table about
his job, and then the guy asks me, and three other people have
started listening. I say, "Ohhh, ummmm . . . I write a Tumblr
called Pitchfork Reviews Reviews." I look down and hope Mike
will say something now.

The guy looks at me for a long second and goes, "Oh, I read
that! It's really funny sometimes. You mean you write *for* it?" I
say, "No, I mean I write it."

"Oh, I thought a bunch of people wrote it. It's like thousands
of words a day." I say, "Nope, it's just me. I'm really into it so it
doesn't feel like writing that much. It really just comes out."

"What's your name?"

"David."

"No, I mean your full name."

"I don't want to be weird, but I'd prefer not to say right now,
maybe another time."

An unidentified girl with thick tortoiseshell glasses turns to
me and says, "What else do you do? Like, to pay your rent." I
have a few options here, including telling her that my parents
pay my rent or telling her where I work, so I opt for the latter.

"I work at a very conservative institution in downtown Manhattan," which sounds as mysterious and prestigious as I can make it. Mike looks at me, and I gently kick his foot under the table with my foot so he doesn't say anything.

"Like the Republican National Committee?" Lexi laughs and I say, "No, nothing like that."

"Where then?"

"I'd prefer not to say. I like to keep my online life, and my social life related to my online life, separate from my professional life."

She asks me where I went to school and what I studied, and I tell her I studied economic policy at NYU, and then she nods slowly like she is coming to understand something, which means that she probably thinks I work at like Goldman Sachs or Merrill Lynch, which is what people who say they work at "conservative institutions downtown" are generally trying to conceal, especially during the Recession, when it is not cool to work at those places because they seem evil and have caused a lot of suffering. Having people think I work at Goldman Sachs is still better than the truth, and darkly mysterious, but I don't want to talk about this at all anymore so I try to change the subject and ask her what she does. She is happy to explain, but before she gets through her first sentence, she's overtaken by a table-wide discussion about how thoroughly Marty Peretz, the *New Republic* publisher, should be punished. My dad loves Marty Peretz. I stay silent on this one.

31

An hour and three beers later, conversations have splintered, and me and Lexi are talking about blogs and the Internet, and I feel very comfortable around him. Mike is deeply engaged in conversation with a cute girl next to him. Lexi tells me to write more about myself in my blog because it's better when I write about myself than when I write about Pitchfork, and I guess I look a little distressed because then he says, "Don't worry, it's good when you write about Pitchfork too," and then after another beer we talk about our dads.

I tell him that my dad is a retired neurologist from Israel who speaks seven languages and has a Ph.D., but has no social contacts and seems to have been driven insane by Internet conspiracy theorists and now lives like a hermit in the basement of his house and periodically emerges to buy gold or yell at my mom. I say, "The worst part about it is that I think he's slowly convincing my mom about the conspiracy stuff. She doesn't disagree with him enough anymore."

Lexi tells me that his dad was from Ukraine and was a brilliant scientist and professor who died three years ago while pursuing his lifelong goal of reformulating and updating Lacan's graph of desire. I take a sip of my beer and we both sit there thinking about our dads for a few seconds. It makes me upset to think about my dad, the way he is now. I say to Lexi, "I'm so sorry."

32

It is a Sunday morning in June, and Emma is leaving for California in a few hours. I wake up and she is still sleeping next to me, so I check my Tumblr dashboard on my BlackBerry and it has 901 followers, and then I spoon Emma and smell her hair and she wakes up. We make out for a while to show each other that we don't care if the other one has morning breath, then we have unprotected sex because she has never had it before and she says she wants to do it with me if she does it with anyone, then we lie in bed and listen to the song "Your Secrets," from Belle and Sebastian's *Books* EP, out of my computer speakers. She cries in my arms and I try not to cry. We have never said "I love you" to each other, but it doesn't matter, I don't think.

33

We go to the deli and Emma gets an iced coffee. She's wearing leggings and one of my T-shirts. I say, "Do you think you're gonna come back early?"

"I don't know, but probably not since I have a contract." After a while, she says, "Will you stay in contact with me? Email me and stuff?" I say, "Maybe," because I think it might be painful to stay in contact with her and be reminded of her. I ask, "Will you read my blog?" She smiles and says, "Yeah, of course, I invented your blog." She kisses me on the nose, and then she cries again in front of the subway station, and then she gets on the subway and takes it uptown to her parents' house, where she gets her luggage and her mom drives her to the airport.

Three hours later she is thirty thousand feet over Ohio, and then four hours after that she is three thousand miles away from me, and I am sitting in my room in the dark, reading Pitchfork reviews from 2001. I pick up a half of a joint off my desk and light it and smoke most of it and then grab my bike and ride over to Ian's in my T-shirt, stoned. When I get to Ian's, I text Emma, "When I get stoned and bike, the wind feels like rain." She doesn't answer. I text her, "That sounds corny," and then I text her, "I'm stoned," and then I text her, "(obviously)."

34

A week later I get an email notifying me that someone has re-blogged something I wrote. I click the link in the email, and it takes me to a Tumblr called Split Infinitives, and it says "Pitch-fork Reviews Reviews is actually getting kind of good" right above the link to my entry, which makes me smile. Then I look at the About Me section, and it says the author of the blog is Stewart Morrison, a Pitchfork staff writer. I jump out of my chair and run into the living room.

Mike is dozing off on the couch, and I run up to him and tap him on the shoulder and he opens his eyes a little bit and I yell, "Stewart Morrison reblogged me and said that something I wrote was good!" Mike opens his eyes more and looks at me and smiles and laughs and says, "That's great, man. Congrats." Then I run back to my room and email Lexi the link to show him that someone from Pitchfork has actually read something I have written. He emails me back to say that he's very proud of me, and he suspected they would come across it sooner or later. He asks for my phone number and calls me and invites me to a bloggers' reading in two weeks that he isn't hosting, and then he asks me to read at a bloggers' reading that he is hosting in a few months. Lexi jokes, "You're in the big time now," and I say, sort of joking but sort of not, "This is the best day of my life."

I tell him that writing about Pitchfork has been the first

thing that I think has made me feel like I have a purpose in my life, which is a lame thing to say, but it's something that I like doing.

"Whenever I wake up, I'm excited about the day because I will get to write about Pitchfork because there is always new Pitchfork writing coming out and it can always be written about."

He asks, "Would you want to write about music for a living?" and I say, "It seems like there are like twenty-five people on earth who can make a living writing about music, so it doesn't really matter what I want."

I go back to reading stuff on the Internet and then my mom texts me, "r u studying 4 LSAT?" I text her back, "Incessantly!" She replies, "want 2 take in october?" I write back, "I don't think I'll be ready by then," and she replies, "wrk faster!!! time wasting."

35

I walk into work and there is only one security guard working. I am a little late, so I rush up to the screening area and take my iPod and headphones off and put them into my backpack and put my backpack on the X-ray conveyor belt and walk through the metal detector and don't beep. The security guard looks at the X-ray screens as my bag passes through and then when they get to the other side she says, "Can you empty your backpack, please?"

I say, "Please . . . I've worked here for months. You see me every day. I know you know who I am. I work in the file room at the FDPF. Why do I have to empty my bag?"

She looks defiant and says, "I need you to empty your bag, sir," and I go, "It's the same stuff that's always in it, that you see every day: the lint and receipts at the bottom, a magazine, maybe an avocado, iPod, and headphones, et cetera. I'm not a security risk and I'm already late. Can we please just not do this, or do it later?" I'm usually nonconfrontational, but I guess the stress about being late to work and being hot from the subway and maybe confidence from people reading my blog has led me into this.

She stands there and looks at me, unmoved. Two people walk in and put their stuff onto the X-ray conveyor belt, and the security guard looks at them and puts her hand up to communicate to them not to go through the metal detector. She looks back at me.

I think for a second and say, in I guess a high-pitched way that people speak when they're strained and upset, "What even are the security risks in this building? What could possibly happen in this building? What is the worst thing that could happen in this building? I don't understand." Another security guard who was on the other side of the lobby puts down his *Daily News* and starts walking toward us.

The other security guard looks us over and goes, "Is there a problem?"

I say, "This woman has seen me almost every day for almost half a year and still pretends not to recognize me even though we greet each other like every day. I don't understand why I should have to empty my bag. I work here just like you guys."

The second security guard looks at the first to try to ascertain if this is all true. The first security guard looks at him and says, "I saw a possible suspicious item in his backpack."

I say to both of them, "I have had the same exact items in my backpack for months, and none of them are suspicious. I shouldn't even have to walk through that thing every day." I point to the metal detector. "Are you doing this just to mess with me?" I ask her.

The second security guard asks to see my Fire Department Pension Fund ID. I take it out of my wallet and show it to him, and then he says, "You should have shown it to her," and I refrain from saying anything. He remains expressionless and lets me pass. I take the elevator upstairs and rush back into my area in the file room, past Dolores and Tommy. Dolores looks at me and says, "You're late. I have to dock you fifteen minutes." I say, "Okay, sorry, I got detained downstairs," and I continue walking back to my desk and sit down. There is no paperwork to file, so I take out my phone and finish reading and reviewing the day's Pitchfork reviews.

I hear Tommy coming up behind me. He looks at me and says, "You, man," and he pauses and looks down at my Black-Berry in my hands and continues, "always on that phone. What do you do on that?" I swivel my chair around to look at him. "I'm mostly just reading news articles and emailing with friends."

"What do you email about?"

I say, "Mostly about stuff related to stuff that we've talked about before." He says, "Oh, like college stuff. I get it."

I say, "Dude, it's not college stuff. It's like, 'Have you listened to the new Lil Wayne song that just leaked?' and stuff like that."

He looks at me incredulously. "You like Wayne?" I nod. He goes on, "I didn't know you like Weezy. I thought you like that ballerina music." He laughs and lifts his hand up and puts up a peace sign with two fingers and then turns the two fingers downward and points the tips of the fingers toward the ground and moves them back and forth rapidly, to look sort of like a cartoon of a woman's legs dancing, and then I laugh and he laughs again. I think we are bonding. Then he kind of shifts back a bit and says, "So, ummm, so me and Eddie, the security guard on twenty-five . . . We gonna go to that Irish bar down the street after work, and we thought, uhh, you know, you might wanna come throw a couple back with us 'cuz you never chill after work with people at the office here. What you think?"

I am flattered so I say, "I'm happy that you'd wanna hang out with me, but I get off at two thirty, and you guys don't get off until six, so I would have to wait for three and a half hours without anything to do . . ."

He looks a little disappointed and nods and says, "Aight, next time." Then he says, "Oh yeah, also, Mangino wants to see you."

36

I ride the elevator upstairs in dread because I know he's gonna reprimand or fire me for fighting with the security guard, and I get out at the twenty-fifth floor, where Mr. Mangino and the other higher-ups in the Fire Department Pension Fund work. I see Linda Greenberg and try to skulk around her, but there's no way to do that without seeming rude given how close we are to each other, and she says, "David! How's everything going?"

"Fantastic! Thank you so much again. I'm feeling really at home in the file room right now." She says, "Is Dolores treating you okay? I know she can be a demanding boss."

"She's great, we're getting along really well." I wonder for a second what percentage of the words that come out of my mouth are lies and estimate that it's probably about 40 percent.

I walk over to Mr. Mangino's office and sit down in a chair in front of his desk as he finishes typing something into a spreadsheet. He looks distracted, and there is a copy of the *New York Times* on his desk, which makes me think he is secretly more enlightened (or something) than the secretaries here who read the *Post* and complain about crime.

Before he has a chance to speak, I blurt out, "I'm really sorry about what happened downstairs but I just got frustrated because the security guard sees me every day and I know she recognizes me, but she pretends to not recognize me, and today she made me late! And I think she was doing it on purpose because she knows what time I come in every day, 9:30, so she knows that if I see her at 9:31 or 9:33 and she detains me for an extra few minutes, then I'm late and my pay gets docked. I don't know what she has against me. I don't know why she treats me like I am new in the building every day I walk in."

Mr. Mangino laughs and says that he called me upstairs to sign the sympathy card for Roxanna in Pension Payroll, who just had a triple bypass and is recuperating in the hospital. I feel embarrassed but I sign the card. Mr. Mangino says he'll make a call downstairs so that I don't have to worry about this anymore. I thank him and return to my desk and finish my second post for the day. I appreciate that he is looking out for me. It is the middle of June and my blog has 1,756 followers.

I walk home from work with my sleeves rolled up because it's hot. My BlackBerry buzzes in my pocket and I take it out to check my email and there's an email that says, "Hi, I just wanted to say, I've enjoyed reading your blog for a while now — you have maybe the most honest writing voice I've ever seen, and it's immensely refreshing. You just keep writing, I'll keep sending you some good vibes! Thanks, Josh."

I forward it to Emma and to my mom and sit on a bench in the park on Lafayette and Spring. My mom calls me and says, "Did you just send me an email? I got a weird email," and I say, "Yeah, I did." She says, "What is Pitchfork Review Review? Is that your email address?"

I say, "Yep."

"Why do you have a secret email address? Is this something I'm not going to want to hear about? You don't have to tell me if it is, but I want you to be careful — actually, tell me."

I explain to my mom that I have been writing a Tumblr

about a popular indie music website, and she asks me some questions about what those terms mean. I tell her I write the whole thing on my BlackBerry and email it to Mike, who posts it on my Tumblr. I tell her it's like how Nouriel Roubini, one of the most famous economists in the world, wrote a whole paper on his BlackBerry while sailing off the coast of St. Tropez because he was on urgent deadline.

"Has it been interfering with your LSAT prep?" she asks, ignoring Nouriel Roubini.

"Only slightly. But Mom, the blog is picking up readers and I really like writing it every day so I want to continue doing it. I just forwarded you that piece of fan mail to show you that there are people on earth who are enjoying reading my writing. I feel satisfied with myself in a way that I never have before."

"How long have you been doing this?" She talks about this like I'm coming out to her, which makes me feel like I'm coming out to her.

"For a few months."

"Do you use your real name?"

"No, I write anonymously."

"Well, that's a relief. People could disagree with something you write and then come after you, or come after us! You shouldn't ever put your name on the Internet."

She thinks for a second and says, "Do you want to be a writer?" I don't know the answer to that question, so I'm silent and she continues: "We wouldn't have bought you a $200,000 education if you had told us you wanted to be writing about music from the outset. You could have gone to a SUNY." I make up my mind and say, "I have no interest in being a professional writer. This is just a hobby between college and law school, okay? I understand that it's not a feasible long-term career option."

"Okay," she says apprehensively. "Keep it that way."

She asks me for the URL of my blog, and I tell her I'll email it to her later so she can just click the link instead of having to write a very long address down. I make a mental note to delete all of the entries that reference sex or drugs or my parents and to never write any more of them. She sounds genuinely curious for a moment and asks me if I have been getting other fan mail.

"I get fan mail about four days a week, mostly from high school kids, mostly in America, who agree with what I'm saying about Pitchfork or identify with me or both."

"Is there any way to make money off this? You know what Dad would say, right?"

"Yeah, he'd say there's 'no parnossah here.'"

"Could you sell advertising space on your website?"

"It's not popular enough to make significant money by selling ads, and anyway, if I were to put ads on my site, people would think I was cheesy or trying to make money off something that should be done out of love and not for profit, and then a lot of my readers would stop reading me and I would rather have those readers than a few extra dollars."

"It seems like you'd rather have anything than a few extra dollars."

Then she says: "Do they know about this at work?" I tell her that nobody at work knows. I ask her not to tell Dad, and she says that she won't tell him but I should tell him at some point because he is my father and I owe it to him to be honest. At the end of our conversation, she sounds a little sad and says, "David, you should never keep something you're doing from us."

"I know." She pauses and inhales and thinks about what she's about to say and continues, "We hope you know that we love you and we're looking out for you and we want what's best for you. Do you understand that?"

"I do."

"We just want you to have the best career and life that you can, to be happy when you're older, and that's why we make sacrifices for you and try to keep you on the right track. Decisions that seem smart when you're twenty-one, like a blog about an Internet website, might not seem so smart when you're older."

"I know."

"Do you remember when you were in high school and you said that you wanted to be in a rock band and you swore to Dad that you would sleep on a dirty floor every night and live in poverty if that's what it would take to be in a rock band?"

"Yeah, that was a little melodramatic . . ."

"And Dad hid that guitar we got you until you said you wouldn't try to do that anymore?"

"Yeah."

"Aren't you glad we did that now?"

"Sort of. I mean, I guess. I don't know."

"Do you remember what happened when we gave it back to you?"

"I didn't really play it anymore."

"Okay, that's all I wanted to ascertain."

37

Two weeks later, me and Mike wake up and go down to the deli to get coffees and bagels with cream cheese and come back to our stoop and watch people walking down the street in front of our apartment building. Mike says that he thinks my blog is getting better and he thinks he might even read it if he didn't know me. Then we walk inside and pack up the stuff in our apartment, and in the afternoon, my mom arrives and I load my stuff into the back of her car, and she drives me to our new apartment in Bushwick, in Brooklyn. Mike's moving van comes about an hour later and carts his stuff over too.

When I get to our new apartment, I carry the first load of my stuff up into my new apartment while my mom stands on the street and makes sure nobody steals the car. When I get downstairs, she looks around with suspicion. "So why this neighborhood?" she says. An empty bag of plantain chips blows by us on the ground.

"A lot of people my age live here," I say.

"Is there a lot of crime?"

"I know people who live here and they say it's fine. The neighborhood is changing, you know? Plus, I don't look like I have a lot of money, so the incentive to rob me is low," I add, pointing to a hole near the collar of my T-shirt. "And also I'm like six feet tall so I don't think I'm first in line for a mugging either way."

She still looks nervous so I say, "You really shouldn't be nervous. It's fine here."

"You know I can't bring your father here, right? He would say, 'How can my only son live in a hovel?' Then he would make you move home."

"Yeah, but he never saw my apartment in the East Village either."

"I know, but it's just because he hates the traffic and the smoke and the noise. It's not you."

We stand there for a second, looking around.

"Okay, you can stay here, but if you ever want to move back to the East Village, just tell me how much you'll need to do it and I'll put it into your account. Okay?"

"Thank you, but I really think it won't be a problem."

"When you were upstairs I saw a teenage mother pushing a plastic stroller, but also two kids who were dressed like you carrying musical equipment."

"Yeah, it's a changing neighborhood." Then I carry the rest of my stuff upstairs and my mom locks the car and comes upstairs and cleans the windows in the living room and in my bedroom with Windex and a rag. When she's finished, she washes the rag with water from the sink and then comes back into the living room and stands a few feet away from the window and puts her hands on her hips and leans back slightly and admires her work. She says, "It looks so much better, right?" The light kind of comes through. I nod. We walk outside and I give her a hug and thank her and wave good-bye to her as she turns onto Bushwick Avenue and drives out of sight.

38

Mike comes with his stuff, and I unpack my computer speakers and plug my iPod into them and listen to Rick Ross in my room while I unpack everything else I own, which includes my clothes and some books about music and two bags of weed, a glass pipe for the weed, a small bag of Percocet (stolen from a friend's mom's medicine cabinet after she had surgery), and a medium-sized bag of mushrooms given to me by a friend who went to go teach English in Korea after college and couldn't bring them with her, but also didn't want to leave them at home where her parents could find them. I wrapped all of this inside a sweatshirt at the bottom of a box of clothes and books so that my mom wouldn't see or smell it in case she decided to stay for the unpacking of my stuff. It takes a while to excavate. Mike walks into my room and asks if I want to go to that reading tonight that Lexi invited us to, and I say, "Yeah, definitely."

In the evening, before we go, I stand in front of the mirror and adjust my hair. Sometimes it gets into just the right spot and looks exactly right, but then the wind always messes it up as soon as I go outside, so after a few seconds I give up and we walk down the stairs of our new apartment and out the door and over to the subway. The reading is in Tribeca, and we get to the auditorium with a few minutes to spare. There are about a hundred people in the audience. The reading is called "First Kiss."

The idea is that bloggers and some New York microcelebrities each tell stories of their first kisses. A few of the readers had their first kiss at summer camp; others had theirs in high school. Lexi reads a story about having his first kiss late. A fourteen-year-old fashion blogger/prodigy sends in a video because she was invited to read at the reading but she lives in Texas so she couldn't make it, and everyone laughs when the video is on. The last reader reads a first-kiss story that is much more profane than anybody else's. He keeps talking about how the pussy is north of the asshole, and how when you are fingering a girl and you find the asshole, all you have to do is move your hand up toward her face and you will find the pussy. It's hard to tell if he's just telling a vulgar joke or if there's some larger meaning here. This isn't my kind of humor.

After the reading, everyone goes outside to smoke, and me and Mike find Lexi, who is standing with Alexandra, the Slate girl, again. He introduces me to Alexandra and we shake hands. She's wearing a tight American Apparel dress. She looks me over and we make eye contact and then I look down instinctively because it takes more confidence than I have to sustain eye contact with her, and then Lexi says, "Everybody's going to this bar in Tribeca now — do you guys wanna come?" Me and Mike both nod and then we start walking south along Varick Street to the bar. We're a big group of about seventy-five bloggers and other New Yorkers who use the Internet, and I find myself walking in between Lexi and the guy who read the story about the pussy and the asshole.

Me and Lexi talk for a second, and then someone comes up next to him and taps him on the shoulder, so he slows down and walks with the other person. I am left just walking next to the profane guy who read the possible parable about the pussy. He asks me what I do and I tell him I write a Tumblr about Pitchfork, and then I ask him what he does and he laughs, like a big guffaw, and turns to the woman who is walking next to him and starts talking to her about something unrelated. I keep looking at him and waiting for him to turn back to me, but he doesn't after about twenty seconds, so I look around for other people I know, but I don't see any. I take out my phone and check it and read a piece of fan email from a high school girl in California.

When we get to the bar, Mike circles around and then comes back to us, and Lexi looks around the room and points out a short man, hunched over, with curly brown hair and thick glasses.

"That's Stewart Morrison," Lexi says.

"Holy shit," I whisper. "Are you sure?" Lexi nods.

I walk up to him and wait for his conversation to end, and then I slip in and nervously introduce myself to him. He looks at me quizzically and I say, "Hi, Stewart. I, ummmm . . . I write that Tumblr called Pitchfork Reviews Reviews and I wanted to meet you." I wring my hands and anticipate his reaction, and he studies my face and smiles a little bit. "I didn't know you appeared in public."

I make a nervous joke. "How could I not appear in public? I have to appear in public everywhere I go! I appear in public every day."

I say, "I've never met an actual Pitchfork writer in person before. This is really thrilling for me. I was just reading your review of the first Man Man album before I came to the reading, and I feel like you really came into Pitchfork with a class of Pitchfork writers that was sort of a golden age of Pitchfork writing." I pause and add, "I hope I haven't offended you with anything I've written about your writing." I want him to like me.

A woman next to him, who he was previously talking to and has been listening the whole time and has almost started to laugh because I maybe look a little hysterical, turns to me and notes that I talk like my blog. I am flattered that she is familiar with my blog. I tell her I'm supposed to talk like my blog because it's a disappointment to meet people from the Internet in person if it makes you realize that they are not like how they are on the Internet. She says, "Yeah, I was reading an interview with Drake the other day and he said something about kids with cool Tumblrs, and 'then you'll meet them and they're just the biggest turkeys in the world.'" I tell her, "I think I'm more like myself on Tumblr than I am in real life. Does that make sense? Maybe it doesn't . . . ?" She smiles and says she knows what I mean.

Mike walks up to us and introduces himself to Stewart and the woman next to him, and we all talk about the reading for a few minutes. I go to the bar to get a Guinness, which costs nine dollars here. It should have gold flakes in the bottom or something. I rush back to Mike and Stewart and the woman who is with him, and then we split off as I talk to Stewart and Mike talks to the woman. I tell Stewart some of the pent-up things I haven't had a chance to write about on my blog yet, much more than he wants to hear, I think, but I can't keep it in because I've been thinking all of these things for so long and have only recently gotten an outlet to express them, and he laughs sometimes but seems distant or uncomfortable. He is neither outstandingly tall nor infinitely cool, more quietly wise and potentially wily but nervous, like me, and it makes me wonder if I have built Pitchfork writers up in my head and gotten them all wrong.

After he says he has to go to the bathroom, which I guess is code for "I'm ready for this conversation to be over," I thank him for talking to me and say it was great to meet him and then go over to Mike, who says he's about to leave, so we say good-bye and he leaves. Then I realize there isn't anyone I know at the party who I have anything else to say to. I look at my phone and drink my beer and try to make it look like I'm just waiting for someone who went to the bathroom or something, but I can only do that for like three minutes before the people around me must realize I'm alone, so I walk out of the bar.

39

Alexandra stands outside, by herself, facing the street and using her iPhone. I walk up behind her and tap her on the shoulder and say, "Hey, I'm David, we met like an hour ago," and she says, "I remember." She doesn't seem opposed to me standing there.

She takes a Parliament Light out of a pack in her tote bag. I take a cigarette out of the pack I bring to social events and ask her if I can use her lighter. She hands it to me and says, "Wanna look at people on Grindr?"

"What is that?"

"It's this app that men sign up for to see if other men who also use the app are nearby, to meet up/have sex. Here, look." She shows me a map of the neighborhood that we are in, with dots on it, and each dot is a man. Once a Grindr user locates another user in the area, he can see that user's profile and, if the profile is appealing, he can send the user a private message and initiate a conversation that could lead to an in-person encounter.

We stand there smoking and looking at Grindr profiles a while. Most of the profile pictures are faces, some are just abs, one is a penis. Alexandra's Grindr profile picture is a cat's head, and I ask if it's her cat, and she says it's just a cat from the Internet. After we've seen about fifty profiles, Alexandra puts her iPhone away and I ask her, "Do you wanna walk around?"

She says yes. She seems receptive to me, maybe romantically, and I try not to say anything objectionable. We walk toward City Hall Park and talk about how she has been eating bagels a lot recently since she just got back to New York after going to grad school in Iowa, and then how the cinnamon-raisin bagel is a mockery of what a bagel is supposed to be, and how only outside of New York would they have thought to make bagels as sweet as cake.

I ask Alexandra about herself, and she tells me that she's an assistant editor at *Granta*, that she went to Harvard for undergrad, which I already knew, and that she just got back from getting a master's in creative writing from Iowa, which is why she was in Iowa. She taught kids my age when she was in grad school. She also says she grew up on the Upper East Side and went to a private school that I've heard of because it was on *Gossip Girl* and Camilla pointed it out to me when we walked past it one time. Every single one of these things is impressive to me, especially the fact that she grew up in New York, because I grew up in the suburbs and always wanted to be from New York, and I think she can tell. When I'm not in New York and people ask me where I'm from, I say "New York," hoping they won't inquire further and will assume I'm from Manhattan.

Alexandra asks what I do and I tell her that I work at a very conservative institution downtown, which I'm not comfortable revealing because we don't know each other very well and I'm trying to keep my blog identity separate from my professional identity, as I mentioned at dinner at Spain. I say, "It's right around here actually," and she asks what I do specifically at that institution and I tell her that I mostly do calculations and transactions involving pensions. Hundreds of thousands of dollars are at stake. I tell her I studied economic policy at NYU so she can hopefully put the fake pieces together and will think I work at Merrill Lynch. She stops into another bar to use a restroom and I text Mike, "Please don't tell anybody where I work," and then Alexandra comes out of the bar and I put my phone away and we walk around City Hall.

I tell her about the newly installed lights around City Hall, which are this ghostly bright white, and how they're actually meant to replicate moonlight. She looks very pretty under the lights and she nods slowly and looks at them carefully. We walk north up Broadway. The street is almost empty and there are bundles of broken-down cardboard boxes waiting to be picked up on the edges of the sidewalk.

When we get to the L train, she says, "Are you taking this?"

I say, "Yeah, you?" And she nods so we go into the subway and wait for the train and take it to Brooklyn and talk the whole time, and before we get up to her stop, which comes a few stops before mine, I say, "We should hang out again soon," and she smiles and nods and then gives me her phone number and I give her mine.

As the subway doors open at her stop, we kiss really fast. And then she runs off the subway so the doors don't close her in. I compose a text message to her that says, "Neat coincidence: we just had a first kiss after the First Kiss reading." And then I type another text that says, "Wouldn't text so soon under normal circumstances but coincidence was striking," and hit Send so that it will send automatically when I get out of the subway and I won't have to worry about forgetting to send it, but then, before I get to my stop, I delete the outgoing texts before they send because it would seem insane to text her this soon.

40

It's the middle of summer and I'm sitting at work, emailing my second blog post of the day to Mike. Tommy brings me a small stack of papers to file, a special filing assignment wherein I have to file the papers into boxes instead of onto shelves. "I'll get right on it," I say, as if it matters whether I file them now or in 2023 or just throw them all into the shredder.

"Nah, man, take your time, it doesn't matter."

After the filing is done, I text Alexandra to ask her if she wants to hang out at seven and meet at my apartment and wear sneakers, and she writes back that that all works.

41

Then I get an email with nothing in the subject line and the body of the email says, "Hey there — this is Jon Caramanica from the *New York Times*. Got a minute to talk about the site?"

My mind races about what he could be emailing me about. I forward the email to my mom and Mike and Lexi with "!!!!!?" above the quoted text. I think about how to choose my words in my reply to Jon Caramanica so that they communicate a casual curiosity about what he would like to talk about rather than a psychotic need to know everything he is thinking right at this moment, including why exactly he is contacting me, how he has heard about my blog, how often he reads it if at all, and what he thinks about it, entry by entry. He's the smartest and most credible music critic there is. I try a few different potential emails out in a draft that doesn't have his email address in the To box, in case I accidentally hit Send before I'm ready to send it and he gets a half-finished draft of an email with wording that would make him think I am deranged and talking to me would be a bad idea. I finally settle on the casually punctuated, reserved, politely curious, "Yeah what about? Over the phone or by email?"

Jon Caramanica writes back to tell me he would prefer talking on the phone, and I write back, "I actually hate talking on the phone, I have a hard time hearing it and can't concentrate.

I could come to wherever you are to talk about it in person though?" He says that works and tells me to meet him in front of the Barnes & Noble on East 86th Street.

On my way uptown, I try to temper my expectations and tell myself that he is probably looking for a small quote, and that it would be so cool to have a small quote in the *New York Times*. I get to the Barnes & Noble on 86th Street twenty-five minutes early and use the bathroom inside, fix my hair with my hand, and walk around the aisles looking at books. Then I think about how it might not be a good idea to be there twenty-five minutes early, so when the appointed meeting time is seven minutes away, I leave Barnes & Noble and walk around the block (an avenue block), so that I will be between three and five minutes late, which is late enough to indicate that I'm not twenty-five minutes early with anticipation but also am not twenty minutes late, which would be disrespectful. I figure that even if he sees me walking around the block in the wrong direction before our appointed meeting time, he doesn't know what I look like, so it won't matter.

Four minutes after the appointed meeting time, I get to Barnes & Noble and stand outside looking totally casual and then a man comes up to me and says, "Pitchfork Reviews Reviews?" I nod, and he introduces himself as Jon Caramanica and shakes my hand. He is at least six foot six, with a thick beard and mustache and long wavy hair like a lion's mane, wearing a Cam'ron T-shirt and vintage high-top Air Jordan sneakers. I look at his jeans and they seem to be very nice denim. He looks at me for a moment and then says, "Do you wanna go for a walk?" I nod and we start walking west, toward Central Park.

42

I ask him some questions about himself and tell him that I have been reading his writing in the *Times* for a long time and I really like it. He thanks me politely. I tell him I read the *Times* every day on my BlackBerry after I read and write about Pitchfork, and that my mom has been a *Times* subscriber since 1989.

He says, "I didn't know you appeared in public, but I have some friends who saw you out one night. They said they thought you might be open to an interview."

Inside the park, he asks, "Has anybody else been talking to you about writing about your blog? Any other journalists?" I tell him that nobody else has. He asks me how old I am and what I studied in school, and I say I'm twenty-one and I studied economic policy, and I tell him about my plans to go to law school. He tells me that when he was my age he wanted to continue going to school instead of writing about music too, so he started a Ph.D. program, but then he dropped out to write about music. It makes me think that maybe he could see some of his younger self in me. He tells me about writing a thesis paper on rap in the 1990s.

He asks me to explain the project of Pitchfork Reviews Reviews and I tell him that I've read Pitchfork every single day since I was fourteen but that I could never share my opinions with anyone because I didn't want people to know that I was reading Pitchfork obsessively. I say, "Like, okay, so, in independent music culture, which obviously stands against authority and against conformity, everyone's individuality is their prized asset and their knowledge of obscure music is a badge of honor, so talking about liking Pitchfork and reading Pitchfork means that you, like, didn't get a critical memo about your own subculture and you are an inauthentic rebel or clueless or both. I guess I don't know where that places me? I mean, because I read it every day. But also because I know I shouldn't, or something, because reading Pitchfork is like using cheat codes to advance to higher levels of being into cool music, I guess." I am nervous to be saying this to him and I wonder what he thinks of me, but he just asks me to go on.

"But then so one day," I say, "I just decided to let out all of the things I'd been thinking about Pitchfork, and now they won't stop coming out. I can't not write about Pitchfork right now. I'm obsessed with it." I look at his face, which looks curious and interested, but I wonder what he'll do with this information, and also if I seem too crazy to write an article about, but I figure that it's better to be honest with him than to pretend I'm writing my blog as a literary experiment or in a character.

He asks me what I do and where I write. I tell him I work at a very conservative place and that I write the whole thing on my BlackBerry. He seems surprised at both of these things and I tell him it's because I don't have Internet at work, and he says, "Why wouldn't you have Internet at work?" I tell him that it's because I do complex financial calculations in Excel, and if I had an Internet connection there wouldn't be anything work-related I could do on it. "My bosses know I would just waste time if I had the

Internet." I can't really tell if this is a plausible lie, but I've said it a few times before, so hopefully that practice has made me believable.

We head out of the park and he asks me for my name and I tell him I can't give it to him. He says, "How about at least a first name?"

"Okay, it's David."

"I'll try to get the piece through my editors without your name, but can you do me a favor and not just go and give your name to, like, the *Village Voice* in three months? It's going to be hard to make the case to my editors that your anonymity needs to be protected, and it won't make me look great if you release it to someone else."

I say, "Okay, I definitely will not give my name to anyone." I am trying to figure out, from his questions, what the article he's writing is going to be like and how much I will be in it.

As we head back toward the subway, Jon asks, "Would you be comfortable having your photo in the *Times*?"

I think about it for a little while and say, "Yes."

"Why a photo but not a name?"

"Because people in my office don't read the *Times*. They only read the *Post* and the *Daily News*. One guy reads the *Times*, but I don't think the Arts section."

"Okay, that's good to know. There will probably be a photo shoot if this goes through."

I think about the house of cards of lies that my life is made up of, which I've set up, piece by piece, at different times and for different reasons, and whether something like a *New York Times* article with my picture about my blog could knock them down. Could people at work find out what I do outside of work? What if my friends found out what I did for a living? That would be traumatic.

Caramanica interrupts my thought to point out that we are at my subway entrance, and then he says we will be in touch about maybe doing another interview, because this one was just a background interview and he has to run the story by his editors, and we shake hands and I thank him and go down into the subway.

43

I get home from the interview, still wearing my work clothes, and hop into the shower and then change into a polo shirt I took from Mike sophomore year and a pair of chinos from J.Crew and then run downstairs. Alexandra is waiting for me outside, leaning up against a wall and reading a book about the golden age of screwball comedy movies, carrying a big brown canvas messenger bag and wearing sneakers as I had requested. The sun is setting behind her. She looks up from her book and sees me and smiles, and I walk up to her and hug her, and she says, "So, why the sneakers?"

"Because we're going biking."

"But I don't have a bike . . . ?"

"I have two. Let me take your bag upstairs because it'll be hard to bike with such a heavy bag, and then we'll go." She gives me her bag and I run up the stairs with it and bring down my bike and Mike's bike and my backpack, and then, on the street in Bushwick, I teach Alexandra how to ride a fixed-gear bike.

I say, "There's no hand brake because you brake with your feet. When you want to stop moving, just stop moving your feet."

"That seems wildly unsafe."

"No, you'll get used to it and you'll be fine, I promise." I think about the quality of this promise, and then I hold her sides as she lifts both feet off the ground and spins the pedals around and slides her feet into the toe clips. She tightens her knuckles around the handlebars, and I slowly walk forward with my hands on her sides until she has enough momentum to keep pedaling on her own, and then I run back to get my own bike and she pedals across Bushwick Avenue, and she laughs and yells back at me, "THIS BIKE FEELS CRAZY!"

I catch up to her and we ride east as the sun sets in front of us, which looks really sick, and I tell her about why I love riding a fixed-gear bike: "It feels more intuitive and more connected to the road than bikes with gears. It feels very natural and like an almost primordial way of riding a bike. Does that make sense? I mean, once you get used to it."

"I'm not sure yet, I've only been on it for like twenty-five seconds."

I say, "People who ride fixed-gears feel a love for their bikes that's disproportionate to the prices or qualities of the bikes. There's something special about them."

"Something special about the bikes or the people?"

"About the bikes. I mean, about the way it feels when you ride them."

"I can see how that could be true. It feels good to ride. Where are we going?"

"The East River."

Before we get to the river, we stop at a deli so I can buy beer for us to drink at the river, but I forgot my wallet at home.

I walk back outside and sheepishly ask, "Do you have any money? I, ummm . . . I left my wallet at home." This is embarrassing.

"A likely story," she jokes, "but you put my bag in your apartment."

I look at her and exhale dramatically and say, "It looks like we're gonna have to do this sober." She smiles and we ride to the river, past new loft buildings and old factory buildings that have been turned into lofts, and then dismount and sit on a bench on the boardwalk overlooking the river and eat some blackberries and grapes and strawberries that I packed for us. She tells me about working at *Granta*, which entails not very much money and a lot of office work, and I think about telling her that my job entails that too, but I'm ashamed of that so I tell her about the possible *New York Times* story about my blog instead.

Then there's a loud sound on the other side of her, and it shocks her and she drops a handful of blackberries in surprise. When she turns away from me to look in the direction that the sound came from, I inch closer to her in hopes of putting my arm around her if the possibility presents itself. Then a handsome man in his midthirties walks his big bulldog past us and looks at Alexandra for a moment too long, and he seems like kind of a threat because he's a handsome man of eligible age with a bulldog who lives in a nice neighborhood by the water. The bulldog flips out about the blackberries and then for like a minute, Alexandra throws blackberries up in the air near the bulldog, giggling, to see if the bulldog can catch one in its mouth, but it doesn't even catch a single one after she throws about ten. The owner drags it away and it looks like I have nothing to worry about from that guy.

44

We ride back to my apartment, where we check our phones and respond to texts and emails, and then we come downstairs and walk to the deli, where I see a bottle of Smirnoff Ice that I buy and hand to Alexandra. She looks at it in mock horror because she knows she has to drink it because "icing" is a fad this summer. I've had to drink Smirnoff Ices out of fear of being perceived as uptight or not a fun guy who would play along. She drinks it. I buy us each a 40 oz. of Coors Light because right off the bat, it's important that she knows I am the kind of guy who drinks 40s, not like wine or craft beer or stuff like that. We go upstairs and look out my window and talk and drink 40s and watch trucks barreling down Bushwick Avenue, clanking and sometimes sparking against the uneven pavement. Then I sit down on my bed and she sits down next to me, then I put my hand on the side of her face and pull her closer and we make out, then we lie down and make out, then we take our shirts and pants off. I kiss her neck and it tastes very salty and sweaty. I wonder if I taste equally salty or if I smell bad and maybe I should go into the bathroom and brush my teeth and put on another layer of deodorant, but she might think, "Did he just surreptitiously put on another layer of deodorant in anticipation of sex? That was weird."

We have sex for about fifteen minutes, which I'm happy with

because sometimes it's not nearly that long, but fifteen minutes isn't so long that she might have been bored, I hope, especially since it was the first time, and then we lie next to each other, a little sweaty because it's summer and I don't have air-conditioning. She kisses me on the shoulder, then points out a bug that is flying around above us, and I tell her I'll close the window. "I hate bugs, they're so fucking disgusting," she says. "Especially bedbugs. Do you have bedbugs?"

"I don't have bedbugs."

"Are you sure?"

"I am totally positive," I say.

"Because, you know, they're huge this year."

"You mean physically huge?" I ask. "Like they've grown? Or just more popular?"

She smiles and says, playfully, "Shut up." Then I get up and put boxers on and go to the bathroom, and then I walk back toward my room and see Camilla with no pants on, closing the door to Mike's room. She hears my footsteps and turns around and squints at me because she doesn't have her glasses on, and we wave at each other. While Alexandra goes to the bathroom I put the rest of my clothes on, and when she comes back in she says, "Why'd you get dressed?"

I say, "Because it's only nine thirty. Let's go do something."

She says, "What do you wanna do?" I tell her I want to walk around my new neighborhood and explore it.

While we walk, Alexandra tells me she's best friends with Lexi, and has been since right after college, but they have no sexual history, which is a relief because he's much taller and thinner than me and went to Yale. She tells me about her other friends too: Julie and Alex, who went to Harvard with her and now work at the *New Yorker* and a law firm respectively, and Amelia, with whom she went to high school and who is in graduate school at Columbia. I tell her about Ian and Mike, who went to NYU with me and now work at a catering company and blog part-time respectively, and Camilla, who is not working at the moment. I don't think she perceives a status gap between her friends, who are successful after college, and mine, who are less successful, or thinks about the world like that. I'm glad she doesn't and I wish I didn't either.

As we approach an especially gloomy corner, we hear loud banging and thrashing music. We see about seventy-five crust punks standing in front of a Mediterranean restaurant with an open black door next to it, and Alexandra says, "Let's go to whatever that is," so we cautiously proceed to the black door and peep around. Alexandra holds my hand. There is a punk show going on inside, and we go up to a man next to the door who looks like he's selling tickets, and I say, "Hey, could we go inside?"

He says, "Sure, but it's over in ten minutes. I won't even charge you." I thank him and we walk inside holding hands, and we're inside a small room with black walls and a stage, and there are four guys on stage wearing black leather gear. One is shirtless and has nipple rings, and they all have tattoos, and the drummer is slamming the drums as hard as he can and the singer is screaming a guttural scream at the top of his lungs and the guitarist is banging on the strings with his open palm, and I turn to Alexandra and she is smiling and taking the whole thing in.

I notice that everyone else in the room is male and nodding along intensely, and I take my phone out and open the Memo-Pad and type into it, "Stop smiling or they will kill us." She looks at me and laughs and takes the phone from me and types, "Why?"

I take it back from her and type, "Because they're punks and we're hipsters and real punks hate hipsters — we're like yuppies to them."

She smiles at me again and then forces her face into expressionlessness and focuses on the show. After the show ends, we walk outside and look at some of the fixed-gear bikes that punks at the show have chained up to a sign on the corner, and they are beautiful all-black fixed-gear stallions with the choicest components. We walk back to my apartment and go upstairs and have affectionate sex, and I wonder if there's something wrong with her that I haven't discovered yet that prevents her from being with someone better than me.

45

On the afternoon of my twenty-second birthday, July 8, my Tumblr has 1,999 followers. I clock out of work using a newly installed electronic handscanning/fingerprinting system that ensures that people can't steal time from the Pension Fund by leaving work early or coming in late.

I walk up to Union Square Park and sit on a bench in the shade because it is sweltering hot. I wish I could wash my face. I call home. My mom answers and says, "David! Happy birthday!" I say, "Thanks, Mom." She says, "Are you enjoying your birthday so far?" I tell her I am because it's a beautiful day and I bought a special cupcake for myself for lunch and ate it at my desk and nobody bothered me, and then she asks what I am doing tonight for my birthday and I tell her that I am being interviewed by the *New York Times* about my blog and then I'm going to hang out with this girl Alexandra that I'm seeing. My mom is silent on the phone for a second, and then she starts speaking slowly, and she says, "David, we are proud of you."

I say, "Thanks, Mom! I appreciate you putting up with me. I know I am an expensive thing to have to deal with and support financially, probably in perpetuity . . ." It's easier to be self-deprecating than to accept a compliment or loving sentiment any other way. There's probably a term for this preference. "Can I talk to Dad?" I ask.

"Yes, he wants to speak to you," she says, putting the phone down to get my dad. In Union Square, a squirrel scampers past my feet, and I think about how it must be really hot in that thick coat in the summer. I think, "Shouldn't it go deep underground or something, like where it's cooler? With a coat like that? I don't understand."

My dad picks up the phone and says, "Duvie?" which is what he calls me when he's being familiar, and I say, "Yeah, hi, Dad! How's it going?"

He speaks slowly and tenderly and says, "Good. Happy birthday. Mom told me about the *New York Times*. I think, generally, this newspaper is all propaganda . . ." My mom whispers something pleadingly in the background, but I think she doesn't need to because he definitely knows what he's about to say, but she's just making sure he doesn't go off message, and he continues, "But for you, you know . . ." He pauses and thinks about how he will phrase the next thing he says, and continues, "This is good."

I walk up to the *New York Times* building on 40th Street and Eighth Avenue, and Jon Caramanica meets me outside the building. We talk about the forthcoming M.I.A. record, which everyone agrees is no good so it's easy to talk about, and then we walk into the *Times* building. The lobby is massive and open and the ceiling is probably about a hundred feet high. We walk into an elevator and he asks me how my day is going, and I say, "It's been good so far. It's actually my birthday," and he says, "Happy birthday! I'll try not to take up too much of your time so you can go out afterward," and I tell him, "Honestly, this interview is like the ultimate thrill of my life, so if you wanted to prolong it, that would be fine too."

He smiles. I feel a little shaky because I am nervous about saying something idiotic and then he will quote me saying something stupid in my first and last appearance in the biggest newspaper in the world, but I am also calmed by the thought that the *New York Times* isn't in the business of digging up indie music writing Tumblrs with two thousand followers to trash them.

46

Jon Caramanica leads me into a conference room and opens the blinds and closes the door and takes out a small voice recorder and puts it on the table in front of him.

"Do you, like, have a list of questions or something?"

"Nope. I find that the best questions and answers come out of organic conversation, so we're just going to talk for a while." I like this approach and think it sounds wise, and also like a therapist's appointment. He asks me many questions about myself and I tell him as much as I can, and sometimes I can't formulate a satisfactory answer to a question in my mind, so I sit there for a while making contemplative sounds and cracking my knuckles, and then he mercifully just moves on to the next question. I ask him some questions about himself too, because we're having an organic conversation, and he tells me that he grew up in Sheepshead Bay and that he is thirty-seven. Sometimes after I ask him a question, he turns his voice recorder off and answers the question and then turns it back on. We talk for a little less than three hours.

At the end of our interview, he turns the voice recorder off for good and I say, "Okay, so how did I do? I hope I didn't sound like a total contradictory idiot with a mind full of conflicting ideas and not realizing it," and he smiles and says I did fine.

He asks if I want a tour of the building, I guess because I

seemed enamored by it when we walked in, and I say I do, so we walk around some of the floors of the New York Times building. The building is mostly empty because people have gone home because it is 8:00 on a Thursday night. He asks me if I want a copy of a section of the newspaper for five days from now, and I nod so he picks it up off a stack of them and hands it to me, which makes me feel like I'm in an elite club for five days. On one floor we stand over a balcony and look down on the international newsroom, which is the most bustling part of the building right now because news is still happening in other parts of the world.

We step back from the balcony and walk over to some big tables, and he shows me blown-up pages of a New York Times that hasn't been put together yet, with text in boxes and spaces for photos and everything in its right place, except that when I look closely I can see that all of the text is gibberish words. I say, "What are those gibberish words?" He says it's called Lorem Ipsum, which is a text that designers and publishers use so they can put together printed materials if they don't have the exact text yet. He says it's a famous block of Latin writing with a lot of the words purposely messed up so it's nonsense, even in Latin.

We walk out of the Times building and talk about Pitchfork writers that we like and don't like. Then we reach the corner of 41st Street and Seventh Avenue, and I am heading south and he is heading north, so we shake hands again and I say, "Do you know when this piece might come out?"

He says, "Probably next Wednesday. I'll keep you posted."

I try to think about possible different things that could happen, and what will change for me, if the story comes out.

I start walking downtown and call my mom and she sounds excited on the phone and she asks how the interview went and I tell her it went well, I think, but I'm not sure because I said a lot of stuff that I don't really remember now because it was three hours long and he was asking incisive questions, and he got it all on tape and I'm worried some of it might not make sense. She says she's sure it won't matter. Then I call Alexandra and we arrange to meet a few blocks south of where I am.

47

Alexandra is waiting for me in Herald Square, and she asks me excitedly how the interview went and I tell her what I told my mom. She is wearing the tight black American Apparel dress again and white slip-on sneakers. She looks pretty today, which I'm thinking about telling her, but then she says, "Happy birthday! I got you something!" I didn't know what she would do in this tricky situation; we haven't really been seeing each other long enough to warrant a gift that's any greater than a token gift, and if she got me a big gift, it might be her way of saying she wants to increase the seriousness of our relationship/nonrelationship, and I don't know if I want that yet.

But on the other hand, if she hadn't gotten me anything at all it also would have been weird, even if only because we are spending my birthday night together and when you spend a birthday with someone who you are having sex with, you should at least get them a present because you are an important person in their life if they are deigning to spend their birthday with you and having sex with you.

So I am thinking about the ramifications of Alexandra's gift as she reaches into her big brown canvas messenger bag and pulls out a smaller bag and does her best to keep it upright. I say, "Should I open it now?" I don't like opening gifts in front of the people who give them to me because I have to look ecstatic about the gift no matter what it is, and I pray this is a gift I will like so I can genuinely smile and won't have to force a smile.

She nods and I look inside and it's some Australian licorice and a Venus flytrap! This is a good gift. A plant that eats bugs. It's perfect because it's probably just the right price and I don't already have one. I smile for real and hug her and thank her, and I think she is happy I like her gift. I put the Venus flytrap in my backpack and we start walking downtown and she asks me, "So what do you want to do tonight?"

"I don't know," I say. "I know Lexi and Mike are seeing the Woody Allen movie that's getting projected on that outdoor screen on the other side of the river in Brooklyn — you wanna walk to that?"

"Sure. It's your night."

"I'd also like to get really fucked up on the way. Could you put up with me getting really fucked up? The worst thing that could happen is that I get really quiet, since I'm not a boisterous drunk, and then really sleepy. But I wouldn't start yelling crazy stuff. I won't do it if you don't want me to."

Alexandra thinks about this for a second and then gives me her permission. "Do you wanna go to a bar?" she says.

"No way, too expensive."

"But it's your birthday."

"I'll have more birthdays and hopefully I will have more money on them, and then I will be able to enjoy drinking in bars more. For now, let's do it my way."

We walk toward the discount liquor store on 29th and Third, and I think about Emma for a second. I miss her. I wonder where she is right now and what she's doing and if she's dating someone else, and if she misses me or thinks about me. I imagine her naked. I wonder if she is wearing overalls and boots and stepping through mud or high grass. We haven't spoken since she left because, like, what's the point? I hope she likes what she is doing in California, living and working on a farm, and also I hope she is not having sex with someone else at this moment. I don't know why I am so possessive.

I look at Alexandra and I feel guilty for a second, and she looks at me quizzically and says, "What is it? You look like you're thinking something serious."

"Oh no, I was just reconsidering something stupid I said in the interview . . ."

We go into the liquor store and I ask the guy behind the counter for a small bottle of Jack Daniel's, and I pay for it with cash because I don't want my parents to see me buying liquor with the debit card connected to the account into which they deposit money, even though it's the same money in the end. At a Duane Reade across the street I buy a 20 oz. Diet Coke and put both of the bottles in my backpack. Then I walk into the bar next door and into the bathroom and go into the toilet stall and close the door behind me. There is a man two stalls away from me, so he can hear what I'm doing, but the sound is muffled by noise coming from the bar.

I very slowly twist open the cap of the Diet Coke bottle to minimize the hissing sound, pour about half the bottle of Diet Coke down into the toilet, making sure to pour from pretty low over the bowl so there's no splashing. Then I fill up the Diet Coke bottle with Jack Daniel's. Then I screw the cap back on the Jack Daniel's bottle and gently place that empty bottle on top of the toilet to minimize the clicking sound. Then I put the bottle of half Diet Coke and half Jack Daniel's into my backpack and stroll out of the bathroom and through the bar and out the front door of the bar. Alexandra is smoking a Parliament Light outside and we walk about half a block and then I take the 20 oz. bottle out and start drinking it and we set off on a walk to Brooklyn.

On the Manhattan Bridge, I am extremely drunk, Alexandra is a little drunk, I think, and we look out across the river. It's twilight, or maybe a little after. The windowless Verizon building stands out like a big beige middle finger in the Manhattan skyline, and I tell Alexandra that big telecommunications buildings, like the Verizon building and the AT&T building on Church Street, don't have windows because they are filled with computer servers, and computer servers have a lot of big fans cooling them because they get really hot, but dust gets in fans and clogs them, and dust also gets into computer servers and clogs them too and sometimes lights on fire, so the buildings are built without windows to prevent or slow the entry of dust from outside. Alexandra tries to seem interested because it's my birthday, but I don't know if she cares about the logic behind the architecture of telecommunications buildings, but she probably does because she's a curious person.

I can see the building that I work in and it looks cool in this light. It used to be the tallest building in the world. We continue across the bridge, and when we get to Brooklyn, I use Google Maps on my phone to get directions from where we are standing to the movie screening. We walk over and people are streaming out of it because it's over, but eventually we find Lexi and Mike outside and we ask them how they liked the movie and they both complain that their backs hurt because they were lying at weird angles on the grass. I say, "That's really befitting of a Woody Allen movie." Alexandra takes me home in a cab, where I finish the liquor, and I fall asleep with my clothes on, but I imagine she kissed me good night.

48

I clock into work at 10:02 and my head hurts. I walk past Dolores at her desk, and she scrutinizes my face and hair and gives me a look indicating that she suspects my hangover but isn't positive about it. She says, sternly, "You're gonna get docked a half an hour," and then her face changes so she doesn't look stern anymore and says, with a little bit of sympathy, "But it's outta my hands now, you know, with the new system?" I nod and say, "Yeah, I know, I'm sorry I'm late. I had a late night last night because it was my birthday . . ."

She looks surprised and says, "Oh! Happy birthday! How old are you now?"

"I'm twenty-two."

She looks surprised again and says, "You're only twenty-two? I thought you were older? About twenty-five or twenty-six at least. It's the beard and the glasses, I think."

I say, "No, twenty-two."

"That's how old my grandson is . . . ," she says reflectively, and then looks me over again and then says, "There's a big pile today. But"— she pauses —"how about you, ummm . . . Why don't you go eat breakfast? You don't look like you've had breakfast and you probably need one today." She smiles and goes on, "You can eat at your desk and you don't have to clock out. Or you can eat it wherever you get it."

I wish I could accept her offer, but I have a blog entry that should be up by 11:00 and another one that should be up around 1:45, so I say, "Is that offer transferable to a late lunch?"

"Yeah, anytime today. And next year on your birthday, same thing. But hopefully you won't be working here next year on your birthday!" She laughs but she says it kindly, so I think she is referring to me being overqualified, not hinting at her disdain for working with me. Four hours later, before I leave for a quick lunch, I ask her if she wants anything and she asks for a toasted, buttered blueberry muffin and then hands me three dollars for it. I come back from lunch and realize that Tommy isn't there, and hasn't been the whole day, and I ask her where he is and she laughs and says, "He probably had a late night too!" She winks at me. Today is the most we have ever talked in my seven months of working for her.

49

On Sunday morning, I wake up early and shower and put on my nice shirt and nice pants, and then a *New York Times* photographer buzzes my apartment and comes upstairs. He is a British man in his late twenties or early thirties and he spends about ten minutes trying to figure out exactly what it is I do, and then he takes pictures of me in different positions around my bed and my room, some holding my BlackBerry and some where I'm not holding it, some with my face obscured and some with my face in plain sight. I've never been in a photo shoot before and I realize it's hard to pose for hundreds of pictures and keep a genuine smile on my face without having it turn into a grimace, so my face gets strained, and it's around a hundred degrees outside and inside so I am sweating and I hope the camera doesn't capture the beads of sweat rolling down my forehead and onto my nose. I have to keep toweling off.

Then we go outside and he takes photos of me that are supposed to represent a blogger in his natural Brooklyn habitat. He says the *Times* prefers natural photos to posed photos. We end up in a concrete schoolyard next to my apartment building, and there are some little kids running around and playing and they ask the photographer if he can take pictures of them, so he takes some pictures with the kids in the foreground and me in the background, and then one of those becomes the picture they use, and it's taken from far enough away so that you can't see the sweat. When we finish shooting, he asks me what I would like to be called in the photo and I say, "'David, a blogger,' I guess?" In the newspaper it appears as "the blogger David," which doesn't really sound right.

50

Two days later, I'm on Tumblr at my desk in my apartment, and I hear a gunshot and then a car speeding away and I stand up and walk over to the window and look outside. A kid who looks like he is high school age is limping away from the concrete schoolyard where my photo was taken by the *Times* photographer. He limps to the deli under my apartment building because he was shot below the knee and needs an ambulance. There are two other kids helping him walk, and one looks terrified and the other looks angry. I call Mike over and he comes and looks at the wounded kid out the window and we watch him limp down the street.

"Should we go help him?" Mike asks. The kid walks into the deli. I say, "I mean, I would like to help him, but I don't know exactly what we could do for him now? I'm sure one of his friends or the guy at the deli is calling the cops and/or an ambulance." Mike shrugs and nods and says, "Fucked up," and then he goes back into his room and goes back on the computer.

An hour and a half later, I am responding to a piece of fan email, and Jon Caramanica calls me and says that the story is going online in an hour and coming out in the paper tomorrow, but the editors have really thought about it and they will need my full name to do some sort of background check on me and verify that I am in fact who I say I am. He says they won't print the name, so I give him my name, and he thanks me, and I thank him again. I look around in my apartment and think I should do the dishes. Jon Caramanica says, "I hope you get what you want out of this." I tell him that what I want to get out of this is to legitimize my blog to my parents enough so that they allow me to push off going to law school for another year.

51

The *Times* story goes online and my Tumblr has 2,135 follow-ers. I read the story really fast once all the way through and then slowly again once. It is called "Pitchfork, Music Criticism's Upstart, Grows Up," and it begins, "Early each weekday morning, the indie music Web site Pitchfork posts five new album reviews. Hours later a 22-year-old reader named David downloads them onto his BlackBerry, reads them on his way to work and muscles out a rambling but surprisingly fluid response using his phone's MemoPad function: no links, no capital letters at the start of sentences, just adrenalized response." The big picture at the top of the page is a picture of Pitchfork founder Ryan Schreiber sitting at his desk, and then there is a small picture of me on the sidebar, which is in accordance with the natural order of things. The story is about both what I do and the rise and current prominence of Pitchfork, and how there are people who are young and into music who don't remember a time before Pitchfork. The implication is that Pitchfork, once a child in music criticism among big magazines and stuff, has grown up and had a child of its own, which is me. I read the story over and over.

I smoke a cigarette and look out the window. It's quiet out-side. Alexandra calls to congratulate me and Mike walks into my room and gives me a high five and then walks back into his room. Ian emails me to congratulate me and then I do some of the dishes and try to think of the people I knew in high school that I wanted to contact after college but couldn't because I hadn't done anything with my life, and how I can now contact them because, from a certain perspective, I have one accomplishment. Then Alexandra comes over and we watch a horror movie and have sex and go to sleep.

The next morning, I wake up and my Tumblr has 4,576 followers and I leave for work and grab two copies of the *New York Times*, and my story is on the bottom fold of the front cover of the Arts section, and then on the back cover of the Arts section there is a picture of me that takes up almost the whole top fold. I get on the subway and see if anyone else is reading the *New York Times* Arts section — maybe they will recognize me and whisper to someone else or wave to me — but nobody is reading it. I get into work at 9:15 and go straight to Mr. Mangino's office and wait for him outside of his office because I know he usually gets in around 9:25. Linda Greenberg walks past me and waves and asks me how my day is going, and I tell her it's going okay but that I need to talk to Mr. Mangino about an issue with my electronic time sheet. She says, "Yeah, I've been having trouble with this new system too," and then she continues walking past me and Mr. Mangino arrives at his office and says, "What can I do for you?"

I say, "Can we go into your office please?"

He opens his office door and we go inside and I close the door behind him and see that he has a copy of the *Times* under his arm and he is also carrying a brown bag of food or coffee.

"So what is it?" he says.

I point to his copy of the *Times* and say, "Can I see that?" He looks curious and hands it to me and I say, cautiously, "Okay, if I show you something, you have to promise not to fire me or tell anyone else in the office. Can you do that?"

"I don't know if I can make that promise. Are you in some sort of trouble?"

"No. Okay, look," I say, and I take out the Arts section and unfold it and show him the picture of me, and he looks at the picture and cocks his head and looks back at me, like a character in a movie would, and then he takes the paper from me and I show him where the story is and he sits down behind his desk and reads it and I sit in the chair in front of his desk and wring my hands.

As he finishes he starts laughing and he says, "You are a weird fucking kid," and I laugh nervously, and he says, "I always knew there was something up with you. Always on your phone in the file room . . ." He calms down and thinks for a moment and says, "But there's nothing in this article that would force me to take disciplinary action regarding your position here." I feel relieved. He says, "But, on the other hand, I don't know how much the other directors in the office would appreciate something like this. This is the New York City Fire Department, not . . ." He struggles for a word and goes on, "Not the New School for Arts and Science. You know what I mean? There's a certain image to uphold."

I nod and say, "So can we keep this between us? I didn't want you to see it and be surprised by it." I'm only telling him all of this because I don't know who else he would bring it up to if he came across it himself.

He nods and then says, "If you stop combin' your hair with firecrackers and wearing pants like that, too small," and he looks at my pants and continues, smiling, "then we're all good." I nod and then he sounds curious and says, "So you write this all from work?" I nod and say, "Well, I start writing on the subway on the way to work, but then, yes, from mostly under my desk in case Dolores walks up behind me and sees me slacking off. I do it only when there's nothing to file though."

This is an obvious lie and maybe he knows it, but he smiles anyway and nods and says, "Do you write about work?"

I tell him, "One time I wrote half a post while I was hiding in a toilet stall on my floor because I had work waiting for me at my desk and I had to finish the post by my deadline, and in the post I wrote that I was hiding in a toilet stall at work, but I took the post down because the detail seemed weird and unnecessary." He smiles and stands up and puts his hand out and we shake hands and he says, "Congratulations, David."

I thank him and then walk out of his office, feeling relieved that the only person at the office who could have found out about this on his own is okay with it, and get on the elevator and walk home, and then at noon, my mom picks me up and I come over to the side of the car window and she looks at me and she's beaming and holding a copy of the paper, and we hug through the window and she says, "Congratulations!"

I say, "Happy birthday!" because it's her sixtieth birthday. I get in the car and we drive to the airport. We fly to Miami, where we are going to spend my mom's sixtieth birthday with her eighty-eight-year-old mother, who is in an assisted living facility there, and her sister, my Auntie Sarah, and Ken, the man my Auntie Sarah has been engaged to for nine years. My mom told me to "not refer to him as 'Uncle Ken' until after he actually marries my sister."

When I was younger my mom told me, "They met on Match .com but they tell people they met at synagogue." I say, "But isn't Auntie Sarah an atheist?" My mom says, "Well, exactly. But Ken isn't." My dad isn't coming to Florida with us to celebrate my mom's sixtieth birthday for several reasons, including "Birthdays are bullshit, meaningless ceremony," "I have everything I need here, so why do I go anywhere else?," and "Ken is a mumser." "Mumser," in Yiddish, I think, means "lowlife." Sometimes my dad talks about Ken and yells, "Bylaad sukkah!" which, in Polish or Russian, means something like "motherfucker."

At a cousin's bar mitzvah when I was twelve, during the cocktail hour, Ken came up to me and asked, "So how's your old man?" A few minutes later my dad came up to me and asked me what Ken had talked to me about, and I said he said, "How's your old man?" My dad doesn't understand American idioms so he yelled, "OLD MAN? WHO IS AN OLD MAN? HE IS OLDER THAN ME!" He went up to Ken and demanded an apology, and Ken tried to explain the idiom, but my dad didn't buy it, so they haven't spoken since and my dad refuses to go to Florida because Ken is there.

On the plane to Miami, I play my mom some Belle and Sebastian with my pairs of headphones and the headphone splitter and my mom rereads the *Times* article. When we land in Miami, Mike texts me that my Tumblr has 6,393 followers. I have messages in my inbox from college friends, including a girl I hooked up with freshman year who I haven't spoken to since, an ex-girlfriend from high school, and fifteen other people I haven't spoken to in months or years as well as some that I have. A Pitchfork writer that I have only been emailing with but have never met in person sends me an email to congratulate me. There is an email from a literary agent, a guy who works for a publisher, a guy who wants me to review records for his website, unpaid, but "the traffic is crazy so the exposure will be fantastic for you."

In the rental car driving from the airport, I read emailed congratulations from people who have previously sent fan mail and write back to as many as I can. I call my dad to ask him if he has read the article yet and he said he hasn't read it but he will probably read it later and the picture of me "is very big but why is it in black and white?"

The last email I read is from Emma, and it has no subject line and just says, "My parents called to tell me they saw you in the newspaper. I miss you." I delete this one so Alexandra couldn't see it if I was looking at my emails on the computer and Alexandra was reading over my shoulder, but then I undo the delete and put it into a folder separate from my inbox.

When we get to my aunt's house, Auntie Sarah and Ken come outside to greet me and she gives me a big hug and says "Congratulations!" and then she hugs my mom and says, "Happy birthday!" Ken wishes my mom a happy birthday and then comes over to me and shakes my hand and says, "Welcome to the club!"

"Thanks. What do you mean?" I ask him.

"I'll show you."

We walk inside my aunt's house and I put my backpack down, and Ken leads me into the bedroom he shares with my aunt and opens a drawer and takes out a folded piece of newspaper, a copy of the *New York Times* from 2005. On the second page an article about rising commodity prices and how they impact higher education, Ken, who used to run the cafeteria at a community college, is quoted as saying, "It's been tough on the staff and tough on the students." I read the line twice and look to see if he is quoted in any lines around it, but he isn't. I look up at him and he looks so proud and he looks down at me expectantly and says, "So now you know what it's like! Being in the ol' *New York Times*! It's somethin', huh?"

I nod and tell him that, yes, it is cool, and then I go into the bathroom and email my dad from my BlackBerry, "You were right, Ken is kind of a motherfucker," and I can hear Mom's cell phone ring two minutes later, while I am still using the bathroom. She steps outside to take the call and stands near the small bathroom window so I can hear her conversation on the patio. I can tell she's talking to my dad, and after ten seconds she starts laughing and then says, "Yehuda, what do you mean 'where does he hear that language?' He's twenty-two and you swear more than he does!" There is a pause on her end of the line as she listens to him and then she says, "It doesn't matter if it's in another language, he knows what it means."

We all eat dinner in the grand dining room of Bubba's assisted living facility. It's called the Palace but Bubba calls it the Prison. Old people surround us and chew very slowly. Sometimes food dribbles down their faces, and I guess that just because Bubba is old doesn't mean she doesn't think it's gross too. A staff of cater waiters brings everyone plates of mostly soft foods of the patrons' choosing, and one of the cater waiters looks like she's about twenty and we keep making eye contact.

Then Bubba interrupts our meal, stands up, walks over to my chair, makes me stand up, and then leads me around the dining room and introduces me to about thirty other seniors who are all dining. She goes up to, I guess, every single person she knows at the assisted living facility and introduces me. I shake a lot of very soft and wrinkly hands, and she is told she has a "very beautiful grandson," a "darling grandson," and a "handsome grandson." She beams, and right before we get back to our table after making the rounds, I give her a hug and we stay in the hug for a long time.

After dinner, Auntie Sarah and Ken take me and my mom for a drive down the boardwalk in Miami Beach. We pass big, beautiful hotels, car dealerships, and a bar called Wet Willie's. There's a huge line outside and I try to think about where I've heard the name "Wet Willie's" before, and I remember that it's from the chorus of the Lil Wayne song "Don't Die," where he raps about being banned from Wet Willie's. Lil Wayne lives in Miami so it must be the same one. I Google "why lil wayne banned wet willies" and find a message board post that says, "Probablly cause him and his crew smelt like straight Dank! I bet thats why."

As the sun is setting in Miami and I am riding in the back-seat of my aunt's car with my mom on her sixtieth birthday and the day a *New York Times* article about my blog came out, I think about what's going to happen to me over the next forty to sixty years of my life, like what the rest of my life will be like. I lay my head to the side on the headrest and roll up the window and fall asleep and feel peaceful, and when we get back to my aunt's house, my mom wakes me up and I walk inside and sleep on an uncomfortable pull-out couch in the guest room.

52

The next weekend, Alexandra's friends arrange for a surprise party for her at her friend Amelia's family's big apartment in Chinatown. Alexandra is supposed to get to the surprise party at 10:00, and so I am charged with occupying and feeding and entertaining her until 9:45, when Amelia will call Alexandra and ask her to come over for a minute to pick something up or something.

On the evening of the party, I pick up Alexandra outside of her office in the West Village and tell her, "So I have a surprise for you," and my surprise is that I'm taking her out to dinner at one of those places in Chinatown that has whole ducks hanging by their feet in storefront windows, which we had talked about wanting to go to because there's something uncanny about the dead animals themselves hanging in the window of a restaurant because food in America is so divorced from its origins that it's unusual to see it like this.

I also want to take Alexandra to a surprise dinner on the night of her surprise party because if she thinks she's already had one surprise there's no way she would suspect another surprise immediately afterward.

So I say, "We have some time to kill first."

"Okay, cool, what do you want to do to kill time?"

"Let's go swimming in the Hudson River."

"Are you serious?"

"Yeah, I've done it a couple times. Nothing bad happens physically. That I can detect."

"Okay," she says, hesitantly, and then we walk down to Pier 40 on the Hudson River and walk down the pier and hop over a plastic gate and walk down to a small dock and put our bags down and take our shirts and pants off and jump into the water and swim around for a while and kiss in the water. She spits water into my face. In New Jersey, across the river, one of the neon triangles on top of the building with two neon triangles above it is out. I think about finding the building on Google Maps and getting the building's phone number and calling it and telling the people who work there that one of their triangles is out, but they probably already know.

We hop out and air-dry and I tell her about the two identical buildings that face each other on the river that house two gigantic fans that blow air through the Holland Tunnel and if the fans stopped working and air stopped getting pushed through the tunnels, everyone in the tunnels would asphyxiate and die. She tells me she actually already knew that, but it was nice to hear it explained, and then she tells me that saying "asphyxiate and die" is redundant because asphyxia includes the death, in the way that "electrocute" means to kill by electric shock, not just to give an electric shock. This is an interesting fact. I file it away to repeat in conversation with someone else another time.

We go down to Chinatown and eat a whole duck and then I give Alexandra a pair of noise-cancelling headphones for her birthday. I am worried that the headphones are like the bowling ball in the *Simpsons* episode where Homer gets Marge a bowling ball for her birthday and Marge says, like, "Homer, you want the bowling ball! I don't want the bowling ball." But Alexandra seems genuinely happy about the headphones.

We leave the restaurant and Alexandra gets the call from Amelia and asks me if I want to stop by Amelia's for a minute because we're right near it, and I say, "Really? Do we *have* to? I thought we were just gonna be hanging out by ourselves tonight . . ." She looks pleading and says, "Please? Just for a minute? I haven't seen her in so long," so I agree to go and Alexandra kisses me.

Upstairs at Amelia's, after a successful surprise, I drink some beers and Alexandra introduces me to some of her friends. We stand in a circle of people and talk, I try to adjust my bunched-up underwear without anybody noticing, with my hand in the pocket, but that doesn't seem possible, and then gradually the circle splinters until everyone is having private conversations and the only people left are me and this blond kid who has neatly parted hair and is wearing tortoiseshell glasses and looks like someone my mom would say is "a nice boy" or "a very smart boy."

He says his name is Andy and tells me he went to school with Alexandra and works for the White House, and then I start drunkenly praising President Obama. I mention that it's unfair that so many people hate President Obama because he's yet been unable to turn the United States into Candy Land in his first year and a half as president despite the two wars and the financial crisis–turned–Great Recession.

After about ten minutes of this, Andy interrupts me and says, "Would you like to meet him?"

I laugh and say, "Oh yeah, sure, I'll give you my email address and you can pass it on to him." Then Andy indicates that he is serious and asks for my email address and says that I might have the chance to meet the president when he is in town on Wednesday. I suspect he is pulling my leg but I give him my email address and he thanks me and we go socialize with other people.

53

The next day Andy emails me and asks me for my full name and my social security number so he can do a background check on me, and I call Alexandra and ask, "Do you think I should give Andy my real name and social security number?" Alexandra says I probably should.

He emails me back and tells me to be at a car rental garage on 41st Street the next morning, and I email him back to ask what the appropriate attire would be for the occasion, and he tells me to wear something formal. I find a rumpled suit jacket and sort-of-matching suit pants and hang them in the bathroom and run the shower hot for about ten minutes to get the wrinkles out of the jacket and pants, and then the next morning I post a blog entry saying that I am on a secret mission for the government so I won't be posting today. My Tumblr has 9,850 followers. I call in sick to work and then I take the subway into the city and meet Andy at the car rental place and he assigns me to drive one of five twelve-passenger Ford E-350 vans through the streets of Manhattan in the presidential motorcade.

54

Today the president is doing two Democratic fund-raisers and appearing on *The View*. My van's name is Press 1 and I am instructed to not speak too much to the members of the press in my van, lest I embarrass the administration. I text my mom, "The power to embarrass a presidential administration is in your son's hands." She writes back, "Exciting!!!!!!"

The five vans pull out of the garage and drive down the FDR Drive to the heliport. I've never driven a van before, so it's unwieldy, and the last time I drove a car, it was a Zipcar that Mike rented that I crashed into a small pole. I didn't mention this to Andy. As the vans drive down the FDR, I keep the windows down on my van and listen to Hot 97. Because the windows are opening and air is blustering around in the van, I jam the printed directions (from the car rental lot to the heliport) under my leg as I drive.

The vans arrive safely at the heliport, which is cordoned off by about five hundred police officers and guys with huge rifles, and me and the other drivers are immediately commanded by the Secret Service to step out of our vans, and they search us with their hands and metal detectors. The other drivers are all around my age or a little older, and they all went to Harvard or Yale. The Secret Service also searches our vans thoroughly in what I hear one Secret Service guy refer to as "doing sweeps of the vans," and then we are ordered to go and wait inside the heliport for the president's arrival. At the soda machine inside the lobby of the heliport, I get a can of Diet Coke and drink it and look out at the water. The handlers tell us, about the president, "Right now, he's eating a sandwich at a sub shop in Edison, New Jersey."

In our downtime awaiting the president, Andy explains why me and some other random college or postcollegiate kids are driving in the presidential motorcade. One reason is that the president is here doing Democratic fund-raisers, which are political, so using enlisted military men or policemen to drive his people around would be ethically questionable (at best) because enlisted men are apolitical by nature. The second reason is that it's expensive to fly drivers from DC because people in New York can drive just as well. The third reason is that there is a culture of volunteerism within the Obama administration, and there are days when the president does rallies and there are hundreds of volunteers like me. Then Andy says, "Actually, the president no longer does rallies. He does 'High-Energy Message Events.'" I text my mom to tell her that because I think she'd get a kick out of it, but tell her not to tell my dad because he hates the president and this Orwellian language will fan the flames. I ask Andy for his permission to write about my day on my blog and he grants it, but I suspect he's unaware that my blog is somewhat popular.

I think about what I will say to the president if I get the chance to meet him, which Andy says is unlikely but could happen, and decide that I will probably ask him about Pitchfork and if he listens to indie music. I tell myself not to be disappointed if I don't get to meet him. After about an hour of waiting in the heliport lobby, we go out to the back of the heliport and take pictures next to the president's car. It's a big Cadillac with wheels that look like truck wheels, and someone says that it looks like a car but it is actually built on a truck chassis. It seems indestructible. One of the other drivers takes a picture with me in front of the president's car, and I take a short video of it with a small video camera that Mike lent me, which the Secret Service inspected and determined was not a bomb or a threat. We are ordered to go back to our vans to sit in the vans because the president has taken off in his helicopter from Edison and we have to start driving as soon as he gets here.

As I sit in my van, I listen to Hot 97 and I wonder if, in the course of conducting a background check on me, the Secret Service came across my most significant endeavor in life so far, which is my blog. But my blog is anonymous so there's no connection to my name. But maybe there's a secret government database of all anonymous blogs and the names of their authors, in case an anonymous blogger starts writing things that are inflammatory about the government, so they will know who it is immediately.

I sit in the sweltering van listening to Hot 97. A song by Young Jeezy and Plies is playing, and right as he is saying, "ONE HUNDRED DOLLARS — THAT'S WHAT THE PUSSY COST ME," a meek-looking middle-aged woman opens the passenger-side door and startles me. "Pussy" was bleeped but only the middle of the world, so you could still hear the "p" and the "ssy." I turn the radio off as fast as I can, and she tells me the president will be arriving shortly, so I should start my engine.

I wait for another five minutes and the helicopter lands and I take a video of it landing, and then another middle-aged woman opens the door of the van and lifts herself into it and slides onto her seat and introduces herself to me as Peggy, the White

House stenographer. I didn't know the White House still had a stenographer, or ever did I guess. We chat for a minute and then there is a lull in our conversation and I ask Peggy what kind of sub the president ate at the sub shop in Edison and she tells me, "He got the super sub," and I ask her what's on that sub, and she says, "I assumed it had everything on it." Then she tells me that the prices of food at the sub shop in Edison were quite reasonable and she remembers them, and she reels them off to me from memory, which makes me think she's a good stenographer: "A small bag of chips was fifty cents, a large bag was one dollar, a small potato salad was $1.69, a large was $2.49," and so on.

Several other members of the press join us in the van and a man with a baton directs me out of the parking lot, and we drive up the FDR, which has been cleared of cars. One of the members of the press in my van is a photographer, and another is a *New York Times* political reporter. I want to tell her that my blog was in her newspaper last week because she's talking to me and treating me like a van driver, and like every van driver I am something more than a van driver, but I refrain from mentioning it. We get off the FDR and turn left into the city and drive into Central Park, and the pace of the motorcade has risen because the president is late for *The View*, so we drive faster and faster on the 65th Street Transverse until we are going at least fifty miles an hour and I am so scared I am going to crash this thing and accidentally kill myself and all of these people. There are no other cars on the road, which you would assume would make this whole thing safer but actually just emboldens everyone to drive faster, and every time we hit a bump the van lifts a few inches, and everyone is talking really loudly, and the scenery is screaming past the windows, and my knuckles are turning white on the wheel, and I just want to get on the intercom with the other cars and vans in the motorcade and yell, "Hey, guys, it's David in Press 1! Can you guys please slow down?! Please?!"

We make it to ABC Studios on time, and the president pulls into the lot and then we pull the vans in after him and wait in the vans until we are told we can exit them. Andy comes past my van and beckons to tell me that I can leave the van, and all of the drivers assemble together, and then we all walk into the studio. On the way into the studio we walk past the president's car, and I peer into the window, and there are two bottles of Aquafina in the cup holders and a Ziploc bag of trail mix. The bag is rumpled, like it has been reused a few times, maybe because the president is an environmentalist and insists on reusing his plastic bags, and the trail mix looks like it might have been assembled at home in a large batch and then doled out into bags.

Me and the other drivers go inside ABC Studios and go down into the basement, where about thirty reporters are watching the live taping of *The View* inside a room with a very low ceiling and dim lights. The reporters sit around tables with their laptops, and most of the laptops have extra batteries and special wireless receivers and antennas taped to the back of the laptops with black electrical tape. They look really hard-core, and I think if I were ever a reporter, I would get a hard-core laptop like this. I have a piece of fuzz or dust in my nose so I try to blow it out by closing my mouth and exhaling, but it doesn't come out, so I press my fingers together on my nose, which gets it.

Right before *The View*'s taping is over, Andy rounds up me and the other drivers and leads us to a special area right near the entrance where we came in. The area has a red carpet on the ground, a blue background for people to stand in front of, American flags on both sides of the carpet, and some fake trees next to the American flags. This is the area where we will be taking a picture with the president, if he has time to take a picture with the volunteer drivers.

All six of us, the drivers, are arranged by a handler so that we're standing in a photo-ready formation. We stand there for fifteen minutes, waiting for the president to come out of a tunnel near us. I fix my hair with my hand, which is something I'm usually self-conscious about doing in front of other people, but this is a special occasion. The hair has to be perfect, or as good as possible. My hands are clammy. David Axelrod, the president's senior adviser, comes out of the tunnel and walks past us and gives us a little wave. He is carrying some papers and looks disheveled. We wait another two or three minutes and then I hear a few people coming down the hallway, their voices indistinct because they're speaking at the same time, and then everyone stops speaking except one voice, and it's a midrange rumble, and it's Barack Obama. He is coming toward me, and then he steps into the room we're in, surrounded by Secret Service guys, and says, "Hi, guys!" His voice sounds like it's booming down from a mountain.

All of the drivers say, "Hi!" almost in unison. He thanks us all for volunteering to drive, and then he looks us all over and sees that we are young, and he says, "Are any of you students?" Two of the drivers say, "Yes," and then he asks them where they go to school, and one says, "Yale," and then the next one says, "Yale." He shakes their hands. Then he says, "What do the rest of you do?" He goes up to the third driver, shakes her hand, learns her occupation, and moves on to the fourth driver. He shakes the fourth driver's hand and learns his occupation.

Then he takes a step toward me, the fifth driver, looks me in the eye, and I say, "It's great to meet you!" He says, "What do you do?" I look Barack Obama in the eye and say, "I write a blog about a popular music website!"

Obama thinks about this for a second and pieces it together. He looks at me quizzically. He says, "Oh! Which website?"

I say, "It's called Pitchfork and it's based in Chicago! Are you familiar with it?" I ask him that because he is only forty-eight and he seems pretty hip and he is from Chicago, where the website has been throwing a big summer music festival for a few years. Obama smiles at me and says, "No, but I'll have to look into it!"

Then Obama takes a few steps and walks around behind the five of us and stands next to me. The photographer in front of us takes our picture twice. Then Obama heads out to his car and we head out to the vans, and I get in my van and the members of the press come back into the van and I start driving them to a Democratic fund-raiser on 44th Street and Park Avenue. The streets are cleared of cars and lined with barricades.

On the corner of 44th and Park Avenue, I stop the van again and everyone gets out and goes into a fund-raiser. I wait a half an hour and listen to Hot 97. I text my mom that I just met the president and not to tell Dad because it would just make him mad. She texts back to tell me that she won't tell him but she's proud of me again. I eat a tuna salad on a bagel that I brought. I wonder, "How many different actual tuna fish make up this bit of tuna salad? Like fifty different fish?" I feel selfish about being responsible for taking so many different lives.

Andy comes up to the window of my van and taps it with the knuckle of his middle finger and I lower the window and he looks at me expectantly and I am smiling wider than I can ever remember smiling. I thank him again for giving me the opportunity to meet the president, and Andy says, "No problem. What did you talk to him about?"

I tell him, and Andy says he "didn't think Barack knew about Pitchfork" because his "primary cultural liaisons," his bodyguard and the First Lady's bodygirl, don't seem like they would have introduced him to it. Andy says that on *The View*, they actually asked the president what kind of music he listens to, and he said, "Everything," and they asked him, "Justin Bieber?"

The president said, "No," and Andy jokes that it's because Justin Bieber got a bigger ovation than the president at the White House Easter Egg Roll this year. After Andy tells me this, he makes sure that I know he is joking. I tell him, "It seems like Justin Bieber got a bigger ovation because people at the White House are used to having Barack Obama around but having Justin Bieber there is novel."

Then the fund-raiser ends and we drive to the West Village, where Obama attends a smaller fund-raiser inside Anna Wintour's apartment. Peggy and the *New York Times* reporter stay in the van with me for a while, and the *New York Times* reporter, who lives in Washington, DC, because she covers politics, asks me what neighborhood we are in. I tell her, "Greenwich Village, I think?" I am hesitant because we are parked on Houston Street, so north of us is Greenwich Village and south of us is Soho. She tells me that she ate at a restaurant on this street one time because Frank Bruni, the famous *New York Times* food critic, recommended it to her. She says, "We're friends."

After the event, the rest of the staff comes back to the van and talks about how cool riding around on Air Force One is. Someone says that at the World Economic Forum at Davos, Air Force One totally dwarfed all of the other world leaders' private jets. Then we drive east on Houston Street down to the FDR Drive, turn right, and drive back to the heliport. I drop my passengers off, we all say good-bye, and then I check the *New York Times* on my BlackBerry and the *New York Times* reporter has put a blog post on the *New York Times* Caucus blog, a politics blog, from the back of my van.

55

The next day I get to work and walk past Dolores and Tommy and make a fake coughing noise so they think that I was sick yesterday, and then I email Mike my morning reviews of Pitchfork reviews and a blog post about my whole day driving the presidential motorcade and talking to the president about Pitchfork, and he posts them. I am hoping that Andy doesn't see my blog post because he might not have liked how much I revealed about my day. When I get out of work, I take the subway out to a FedEx warehouse deep in Brooklyn to pick up a package that I needed to sign for, but I missed my three opportunities to sign for it so they are just holding it at a warehouse in an industrial section of Brooklyn. Inside the package is Pitchfork editor Scott Plagenhoef's book about Belle and Sebastian's album *If You're Feeling Sinister*.

I get off the subway and Mike has texted me to tell me that an editor from the *Village Voice* has tweeted, "Pro-tip: when the President asks you what you do, do not tell him that you write a blog about a website." I am a little hurt by this but I try to brush it off. Then I see an email from a *Washington Post* music reporter who used to be in a band called Q and Not U that I listened to in high school, and he says he wants to talk to me on the phone about my blog post about talking to the president. I call him as I walk past factories and warehouses and he asks me some questions about it, and I tell him that I was so nervous as it was happening that "I almost don't remember it." Right after I say this, I realize that saying something like that could really discredit whatever I say. I ask him why he is asking me these questions and he says that an article about this is going to be in the *Washington Post* tomorrow. I thank him and we get off the phone.

56

That night, me and Alexandra are drinking in a bar in the West Village. We sit in front of a window that looks down on the street and pull our bar stools close to each other. We talk about Israel and Palestine, I touch her hair, I drink a Guinness and she drinks a Brooklyn Lager. In our reflections in the window, I can see that there is a pimple near my right temple and Alexandra is sitting to the right of me, so I say, "Could we switch seats please?"

"Why?" she asks. There really is no plausible-sounding reason I can generate here so I say, "I would just really prefer it if I could sit on the other side of you." I just don't want her to have to look at my pimple.

She gives me a strange look and we switch seats and then she gets up and goes to the bathroom and I check my email and realize that I haven't gotten any personal fan correspondence since the *New York Times* article, and Alexandra comes back to the table and I tell her about it and she suggests that it's probably because people think my blog is too popular and that I am somehow no longer accessible or something.

Then my cell phone rings and it's Andy and he is furious about my blog post and he tells me, "You need to take that down. Now."

"I don't think I should because"—and I pause because I

know what I'm about to say is really going to make him recon-figure his whole strategy and make him more furious — "there's a *Washington Post* article about it tomorrow."

"An article about your *blog post?*" I say, "Yeah. It's pretty meta. A newspaper article about a blog post on a blog about a web-site." There is silence on his end of the phone, so I take the op-portunity to add, "And I think that if the post was taken down and there was an article about it in a newspaper, it might make you guys look draconian. People would want to read it even more. There's nothing really damaging in the blog post."

He exhales in frustration and goes on, "Okay, I think you're right. I'm going to email you all of the changes I want made to the piece, so that it remains whole but so that sensitive informa-tion that could potentially embarrass people is taken out."

I try to think about what the sensitive information in the post could even be. I didn't include the part about Peggy telling me that Dick Cheney wasn't nice to her and never greeted her, or the part about Peggy talking about being on Air Force One with President Bush and he put his hand on her shoulder and said, "Trust in me. Believe in me." I think that would have been the damaging stuff.

Andy emails me a list of grievances and I address as many of them as I can while still making the post feel whole, and then the next day I am sitting at my desk at work and I read the *Washington Post* article and part of it says, "A White House official says that 'the broad details' of David's account are 'basi-cally accurate . . . but the way he characterizes and attributes the comments and details is mostly inaccurate.'"

Everything I wrote in the post was accurate but I think I should probably not call Andy and contest it because he already hates me and calling him would do no good. A woman from

Tumblr emails me to say that I wrote the only Tumblr post ever to cause the White House to release a statement about it, and I email her back to say that this has been a pretty wild ride and I am a very lucky Tumblrer so far. My Tumblr has 11,245 followers, and I sit at my desk in the back of the Fire Department Pension Fund and collect $14.26 an hour after taxes.

57

At the end of August, me and Mike and Alexandra and Camilla and Ian stand outside of a bar in Chinatown for the event in Lexi's reading series that I'm reading at. The bar used to be a massage parlor so it's called Happy Endings, and it's dark and very narrow inside. It's humid and I am perspiring again. I am very nervous to read because I have never read my writing in front of other people, and there are some people with a lot of cultural capital on the lineup to read at this bloggers' reading, including Sasha Frere-Jones, the *New Yorker* pop music critic, and Das Racist, a very clever political rap group. We drink Four Lokos out of paper bags and I start to jitter a little bit from the caffeine, but then the alcohol kicks in and I feel better. We finish them and Mike throws the cans away and I say, "A few weeks ago my mom watched a news report about Four Loko and texted me, 'Do not drink 4 loko plz. Not safe.'" Mike and Ian laugh.

My friends are talking to each other, and I run over some of the lines from what I am about to read at this reading in my mind and then on my BlackBerry screen. Two guys who look like they are in their twenties come over to me, both wearing flannels and glasses, and introduce themselves and say they really love my blog, and I thank them and they ask me a question about it and I say I'd like to chat but I have to go over what I'm reading again tonight. One of them says, "We're really looking forward to seeing you read, we came here to check you out," and the other one says, "It seems like most of the people here are here for you," and I nod, then say, "I don't think that's true but that's a nice thing to say," thank them, and turn back to my friends.

Ian says, "Fuck, you're famous now." Mike laughs. Alexandra says, "Some kids recognized him on the street outside Bowery Ballroom yesterday." I say, "That's not being famous."

Ian says, "You're the most famous person I know," and I say, "That's because we don't know any famous people," and Ian shrugs and I think about this for a second and say, "Okay, Michael Jackson is world famous. Nancy Pelosi is nationally famous. That newscaster on Fox 5 with the hair that looks like a plastic wig is locally famous in the biggest media market in the country. The people who host the show that plays on the screens inside taxis are locally famous also. A weathergirl on a local ABC affiliate in a region with very low population density in a state with a very small population is also locally famous, and I am to the weathergirl as the weathergirl is to Michael Jackson." Alexandra and Mike laugh. This seems to settle the discussion.

We go inside and find seats inside the crowded bar where the reading is taking place. I sit next to Alexandra and hold her hand under the table and whisper, "I'm nervous," and she kisses my ear and tells me not to be nervous. Two readers read and I am shaky and perspiring but I feel cold. I yawn every thirty seconds but I don't know why.

Then it's my turn to read. I push through the crowd, about 125 twenty-somethings wearing tote bags from literary publications and food co-ops, and push toward the podium. I breathe into the microphone and it squeaks, and I look up and there's a spotlight right in my eyes and I can't see anything except a white light. Someone in the back screams, "Obama!" Some people laugh. Lexi comes over and yells into the microphone for everyone to calm down, and then he looks me in the eye and touches my shoulder. People stop talking and then I start reading a story about the thing that happened that caused me to be in this whole situation in the first place:

On Valentine's Day last year, me and my ex-girlfriend Hannah went to dinner at this restaurant in Williamsburg. She broke up with me in college but I'd been trying to convince her to get back together with me ever since. After dinner, we took a cab home, and as we're going over the Williamsburg Bridge in the cab, she says she feels something in the seat and reaches into the crevice in between the back of the seat and the seat itself and pulls out a cell phone.

Hannah suggests that we give it to the cabdriver for him to return it and I say that we should, like, at least go through the text messages before giving it back. So we read all the text messages and guess that it is a man's cell phone based on some of the messages. There are some steamy text exchanges with someone named Ariel whose gender is impossible to determine from the name and the messages.

Eventually, the cab drops us off and we decide to not give the phone to the cabdriver because I figure I can probably return it for a reward. I text Ariel, from the phone, "what is the email address of the owner of this phone?" and they text back an email address (with a woman's name) @ an investment bank, so I send an email to that email address that says, "hey, i found your phone in a cab and I want to return it — how do i do that?" The next morning, I get an email that says, like, "hey thank you so much!!!" and this woman tells me where she lives and also asks if I want her to pick it up from me. I say, "no, it's okay, i can return the phone because i will actually be in your neighborhood later today."

We set up a time to meet at her building and then later that day I have lunch in Williamsburg and walk over to this woman's building and buzz her apartment and wait like thirty seconds. She comes outside and looks around for me and I hold up the cell phone to identify myself and she walks over to me and she is smiling. She is blond and in her early thirties, I think, and I say, "Hey, I'm David," because it seems appropriate to introduce myself. I hand her the phone and she hands me a box of cookies, like the kind of cookies that look fancy but you can get them from the deli, and I appreciate the gesture even though you can get the cookies from the deli, and she thanks me a lot.

And then I say, hesitantly, "Me and my girlfriend went through all your text messages and we have some questions," and part of me expected her to freak out and be like, "How could you invade my privacy like that?!" I would have been like, "No, come on, I am returning your phone, thereby saving you hundreds of dollars and hours of wasted time, ten minutes of harmless voyeurism is the least I can expect in return, you know? I wasn't really expecting a reward."

But then she did what I thought was the reasonable thing to do, which was to laugh and say that she would have done the same thing. She says, "Okay, what do you wanna know?" And I say, "Is Ariel a man or a woman, what is your relationship to them, and also who is Melanie and why are you fighting with her?"

She tells me that Ariel is her boss and they have been seeing each other secretly because he is married, and also it's against company policy for someone to be dating their boss, and Melanie is her friend who she is just having an ordinary friend fight with that is not interesting.

I say, "Okay, cool, that's it, I guess," and then she thanks me again and we start to walk away from each other, and then I work up my courage and turn around and say, "No, wait!" She turns around and gives me like a puzzled look and I say, "Your email address is @ an investment bank — is that where you work?" She nods and I say, "Okay, this is a long shot, but I just graduated from NYU with a degree in economics and I currently have a job I don't really like — your bank isn't hiring, is it?"

She thinks for a second, and I guess she is considering how someone who is asking her for a job knows that she is sleeping with her married boss, but it's the same person who helped her out a lot by returning her cell phone, and then she says, "Actually, we are looking for someone . . . Why don't you send me your résumé and I'll look it over?" I must be smiling like a maniac, and then I thank her and walk back over the bridge to Manhattan.

I send her my résumé as soon as I get home, and three days later she emails me back to ask me to come in for an interview. She sends me some literature about the bank and the job and her division, which actually happens to be at the Credit Default Swap trading desk. Credit default swaps are the security instruments most blamed for bringing the global economy to its knees in 2008. A credit default swap is a bet that a corporation or country will default on its loans, which is morbid because a lot of people are financially devastated when that happens. Credit default swaps were originally meant to work as insurance, so if you had loaned Greece $100 million, you could take out $100 million worth of insurance on that loan in the form of credit default swaps, and if Greece defaulted on your loan, you could get your money back from the issuer of the swap, but now people buy trillions of dollars of credit default swaps for debt they don't even own, which has proven to be an inherently dangerous practice for the global economy. But that's what I wanted to do for work.

I read all the literature she sent me, and all the stuff about credit default swaps that I can find, buy a suit at Men's Wearhouse, and go in for the interview with the woman herself. It seems to go really well. She tells me how much the job pays, which is still more money than I think I will ever make. She tells me that she wants me to get the job because I seem good and she doesn't want to have to keep interviewing people. She says Ariel is going to interview me after she's done and he's going to ask me how many golf balls can fit into a stretch limo, and the right answer is to make reasonable estimates on the spot, maybe say, "It's probably like 100 golf balls high by 60 golf balls wide by 1,000 golf balls long," and to look like I'm thinking really hard, and then just do the math in my head and give him the answer. I ask, "Out of curiosity, what would a wrong answer be?" She says, "Freaking out about the question."

I meet Ariel, and don't mention that I know about their

affair. He asks me about the golf balls and I get it right. He nods slowly as I'm talking, like he's really thinking about what I'm saying. As I'm leaving the interview, Ariel says they will get back to me soon if they decide to hire me, and when I get home, I send the woman a heartfelt thank-you email and ask when I can expect to hear from them about the job because I'd forgotten to ask about it during the interview.

And then a week goes by and nothing happens, no response to my email or any other communication, and I start to think he decided he didn't like me and I wouldn't get the job, but I want to make sure, so I send another email thanking the woman for the interview and reiterating my interest in the job and again politely asking when I might expect to hear about whether or not I am hired. I tell her I understand if I am not the right candidate, but that I also think I would be great for the job, but I would prefer not to be kept in suspense if I didn't get it. It sounds weird to say that I sent that email to an interviewer, but my email was friendly and not weird. I even had a friend proofread it for unnecessary weirdness and she said it was fine.

And then another week goes by and I am despondent because I know they had decided not to hire me. I think, like, "I returned this woman's cell phone — the least she could do is send me back an email to say I didn't get this job so I could stop worrying about it constantly," because I was having trouble sleeping and I felt hopeless about ever finding a job that didn't make me dread getting out of bed in the morning.

And then finally, after two and a half weeks without any communication since the interview, I sat at my desk at my current job and wrote an email on my BlackBerry to the woman and sent it and didn't even proofread it.

When I started writing this story, I thought the highlight of it was going to be the email itself, copied and pasted, but I can't put it in because it is too embarrassing and sad. Thinking about including that email in this story is like when you break up with someone and you want people who ask you about the breakup to think you're over it, and maybe you even think you are over it, so you start to talk about it, and then you start getting emotional, and you think, like, "Man, I am definitely not over this yet."

The email had some curses in it and also said some stuff about how her business, trading credit default swaps and collateralized debt obligations and other asset-backed securities, had just destroyed millions of people's lives.

And then she emails me back five minutes later and her email says three things: first, "Seek help"; second, "Thank god you showed your true colors before we hired you"; and third, a series of copied and pasted emails between this woman and the Human Resources department at the bank indicating that they had decided to hire me and she had sent my information to Human Resources. Human Resources was supposed to call me later that day to tell me what the next steps in the hiring process were, i.e., coming in and signing papers. I would have started in three weeks.

I walked home from work that day and listened to "Fuck Tha World" by Lil Wayne and cried on the phone to my dad, who said I needed to go to law school so stuff like this wouldn't happen to me anymore. He wasn't angry or disappointed with me, even though he has high expectations for my life in terms of a return on his investment. He said she should have emailed me back when I asked when I was supposed to hear back rather than never emailing me back, and I thought that was uncharacteristically understanding of him.

Sometimes when I'm at work now, I think about how my life would be different if I hadn't sent that email, e.g., how I would be able to afford nicer stuff and have a secure future and feel proud of what I did every day. Even if it was catastrophically destructive, someone was going to do it. I think the only way I can eventually feel good about not getting that job is if I do something fulfilling or lucrative in the future, so wish me luck, I guess.

I finish reading and I look up at Alexandra. I walk over and sit down next to her and she kisses me softly. The next reader starts reading, and I hope people liked my story even though I was a very nervous public speaker, and I turn to Alexandra and whisper, "I hope people liked my story. I feel like I read it like a robot." She sighs and whispers, "They liked it. Everybody liked it. Did you hear them clapping?" She sounds sort of sad. I say, "I couldn't concentrate on it, all I could hear was people chattering and whispering while I was reading."

She turns to me and says, "Know what your problem is, Shapiro? It's that you just have this really shitty way of looking at things, you know? I don't have that problem. I just look at the dopeness. But you, it's like you just look at the wackness?" I smile. This is from the movie *The Wackness*. But she looks sad again for a second and turns and faces forward and looks down. I am sorry I put her in an uncomfortable position by talking about someone I used to be in love with in public. I think she might be hurt and I try to see her face clearly but I can't make it out.

I rub her back and whisper, "Are you sure everything is okay?" She nods and then looks attentively at the person who is reading in a way that demonstrates that she is focusing on the reading and I should too. I think about saying something else but then I think if I started speaking, she would whisper something like, "Okay, now you're being rude, you didn't want people to talk while you read and you shouldn't talk while other people read," because she doesn't want to talk right now.

58

Two weeks later, Camilla picks me up from work and we start walking uptown on Centre Street and I ask her what she did today and she says, "Shopping. And then I ate. Because that's what I do when I don't have a job and am sick of applying for jobs: shop and eat." It's hard to know how to respond to this, so I nod and wait for her to say the next thing. She says, "How was work?" I say, "I feel like my day doesn't really start until I'm out of it." I think about whether I would have steered my life and priorities in school differently if I knew my parents wouldn't be able to support me ad infinitum, and I think I would have, but it's hard to say exactly how. Maybe I would have been more active in clubs in high school or gotten more internships in college? I think about asking Camilla if she would have geared her life differently if she didn't know her parents could support her, but I don't trust myself to phrase it in a way that wouldn't offend or upset her. We keep walking north and it's really sunny, so I take my hat out of my backpack and put it on, and she puts sunglasses on, and then she stops into a juice bar and gets a vegetable juice, and I stand outside and squint because it's still really bright out, even with the hat and sunglasses on.

She comes out and says, "You know what I was thinking about today? The CEO of McDonald's would probably never eat at McDonald's. He probably thinks it's disgusting."

I laugh and say, "I bet he does eat it sometimes, like whenever they open one in a new country or something, he probably has to go there and get his picture taken at the opening and probably take a bite of a burger and look like he's really standing behind his product."

"Why would he have to do that? Doesn't Ronald McDonald do that? I'd think that McDonald's would want to keep a tight lid on the insanely rich old white American man at the head of the corporation propagating a worldwide obesity epidemic."

I nod in agreement but still wonder if she's right, and she continues, "I bet the closest he gets to a McDonald's is when he gets driven past one." I nod and look at a woman who is walking a tiny dog that looks like a big rat and say, "I just read that Tommy Franks, the general who was running the wars in Iraq and Afghanistan, is on the board of Chuck E. Cheese's."

Camilla smiles and we keep walking, and then she asks me if I ever talk to Emma and I say, "I don't talk to her but I think about her sometimes. I think she probably thinks about me too." Camilla giggles and says, "Does Alexandra know?" I say, "That I think about someone else? No way. I don't think she's even aware of the existence of an Emma character in my life, you know? I think she thinks I've been single since college." Camilla nods.

We sit down on a bench in the park on Lafayette Street and Spring Street, and Mike calls Camilla and she says she's with me but we're heading up to the L train if he wants her to come over. He must say, "Yes, come over," because she says she'll be there in about an hour and gets off the phone.

"What's the deal with you guys?" I ask. "He never tells me what the current status is."

"Yeah, I'd expect that. He lives a really compartmentalized

life." I think about that for a second and wonder if he leads a more compartmentalized life than I do, but I don't see how he could unless he has some really devastating secrets that only he knows about. I think about asking her if he has any good secrets but I don't think she'd tell me. She continues, "We talk a lot but we haven't hooked up in a long time."

On a bench across the small park from us, there are two kids, a guy and a girl, who look like they're about sixteen or seventeen and they are looking at us. The guy looks like he's looking at me but I can't really tell from this distance. He takes out his iPhone and both of them look at the screen as the boy conducts a brief operation on it and intermittently look up at us, and I say to Camilla, "Are those kids looking at us?" She looks at them and shrugs.

We talk for another minute and then the kids get up off their bench and start coming toward us. They are both wearing backpacks and Vans, the girl has headphones around her neck, and the boy has acne scars. They come over to us and stand in front of us, and her head blocks the sun out of my view, and the boy says, hesitantly, "Are you the guy who writes Pitchfork Reviews Reviews?" The girl wrings her hands.

I look up at him and nod and put my hand out and say, "Yeah, I'm David," and shake their hands and then continue, "And this is Camilla." Camilla shakes their hands too and the boy says, "We just wanted to say we love your blog."

"Thanks," I say.

"He used to read it out loud to me!" the girl blurts out. The boy laughs nervously and nods.

"That's great," I say. "I think if I had to choose how it'd be read, I would choose 'boys reading it out loud to girls.'" The kids giggle and then say they'll stop bothering me, and I say,

"You weren't bothering me," and they both shake my hand again and walk away quickly.

After the kids walk away, Camilla says, "That was cool." She takes one of the last sips of her vegetable juice and says, "I wonder if Alexandra is, you know . . . Because she's a writer too?"

I think the word she's missing is "jealous," so I say, "I don't think she is. She gets paid to write. I'm jealous of her."

"Are you really?"

"I don't know. People coming up to me say they like my blog doesn't put food on my family," I say, because one time George W. Bush said, "I know how hard it is to put food on your family."

Camilla gets it and laughs, and I say, "And even if she was, she wouldn't ever express it."

She says, "Yeah, she seems kind of passive-aggressive."

I say, "I guess I honestly don't think she is though. I'm an Internet writer. She's a real writer."

59

At the end of September, I pick Alexandra up from work and I'm in a good mood.

"Honey, my blog was mentioned in *Rolling Stone*! It was just a little thing that said, 'Hot Blog Idea: Pitchfork Reviews Reviews Reviews,' but isn't that cool? Some guy emailed me to ask me if I'd seen it and I said I hadn't and he took a picture of it with his phone and sent it to me. Can we pick up a copy? I want to show my parents." She says, dryly, "Sure." She keeps walking and we don't say anything for a long time, like four blocks. I am hungry for a snack so we stop at the cart that sells hot meats on skewers on 14th Street and Fourth Avenue, in front of the Best Buy, and I ask the guy behind the cart for a skewer of chicken. He hands me four pieces of chicken inside a hot dog bun and I pay and then I pick a piece of chicken out of the bun with my hand and start to eat it, avoiding the carbs in the bun. We start walking away from the cart, toward Union Square, and I turn back around and look at the cart, and it's emitting huge plumes of smoke, like it always does when it's in use. I turn around and look straight ahead and say to Alexandra, "Okay, what do you think is responsible for a greater contribution to harmful gases in the atmosphere, but only coming from New York City: cigarette smoke or the smoke from street meat carts?"

She says, "I don't know," and I think for a moment and say, "I know, nobody knows, but what do you think?" She says, "Actually, somebody might know. Somebody who measures that type of thing. I, personally, do not know and haven't thought about it enough to form an opinion. It's a pointless question." Then she is silent and we continue walking toward Union Square and sit down on a bench. The sun is going down.

I say, "Is everything okay, honey?" She leans forward and puts her elbows on her knees, so I can see the back of her head, and she looks around for a while, and I pick another piece of grilled chicken out of the bun and start eating it. Then I finish eating that piece and lean forward too so my face can be next to hers. She looks away from me, and then she turns back and looks at me. Her eyes are a little red and her lip is quivering, and a small tear rolls down her cheek, like the Indian chief in those old commercials about littering. I am concerned.

"Is it because I read about that ex-girlfriend in that story I read at Lexi's reading? I didn't mean to embarrass you by talking about another girl. It was just part of the story." She shakes her head slowly and another tear comes down her other cheek and the first one falls onto her dress.

"I can't hear about your blog anymore. And your career and success and everything all the time." She sobs, and then she sobs again more loudly, and I nod and say, "Okay, I won't talk about it," and put my arm around her, and move closer to her, and kiss the back of her head, and her hair smells like a person, not a shampoo.

I say, "If it's any consolation, none of my writing pays. I have no significant, likely prospects for a paid writing job."

She doesn't say anything. I say, "My success qualifies me for no jobs or money. I don't think people take me seriously. Most of the people who would be able to pay me for my writing dismiss it offhandedly because it is mostly rants about a music website and indiscreetly emotional stories about not being able to grow up, as told through indie music lyrics. I also have no genuine interest in doing what I promised my parents I would do, which is go to law school, and no plans for my future besides that. So 'success' is really maybe not the right word here."

She is smiling so I continue, "At least you have a job in a field related to what you want to do, which is be a writer."

She laughs and smiles and says, "I make $32,000 a year! And I have a graduate degree!" I wish I could tell her I make $13,689.60 a year. I say, "But there's a thousand more things you're qualified to do too. You could teach and stuff."

She says, "We are, like, really well-educated failure machines."

We both smile at each other and kiss on the bench. She isn't crying anymore but her eyes are still red. I wish I could tell her that I work at a clerical job and have been lying about it to everyone for months because I'm embarrassed about it. She takes one of my pieces of grilled chicken out of the hot dog bun and starts eating it, and I eat the last one and throw the hot dog bun into a patch of grass behind us.

A pigeon struts by quickly with another, larger pigeon strutting behind it, trying to catch up with it and have sex with it. The first one is trying to avoid having sex. Then they see my hot dog bun and it distracts them both, and they run over to the bun and eat it together. I point the whole thing out to Alexandra and say, "A moment of cooperation among these tiny fowl."

"Pigeons aren't fowl."

"They're not?"

"I don't think so."

I think about how pigeons are sort of like small chickens, and I try to imagine how small the pieces of chicken that we are eating would be if they were made from a proportional amount of pigeon.

I say, "Imagine pigeon nuggets."

Alexandra says, "Or popcorn pigeon."

I laugh and say, "They would probably be the same thing!" We sit there for a while, looking out at the people on the grass and the sunlight coming through the spaces between the buildings.

I say, "Does the fact that a pigeon is also a type of dove diminish the status of the dove or elevate the status of the pigeon?" This reminds me of a sample LSAT question that I saw on the back of the LSAT prep book. Alexandra says, "Why can't both be true?"

60

The next day, I am in the file room, putting away a stack of loan applications that were just sent down from Loans upstairs. Some days, when I am satisfied with my posts and I feel like I'm close to being in my right place in the universe for the moment, which is sort of fleeting but it comes sometimes, filing becomes not exactly fun but less debasing than usual. Posts don't come as easily as they did when I started, so a good one feels extra good right now. So sometimes, I imagine filing like it's a very regimented ballet, or like a concentration game, or like my life depends on getting the right file in the right folder and if I don't, Mr. Mangino will come downstairs and tell Dolores that I'm no longer allowed to use my BlackBerry on work time.

Also, other times, when there is really nothing to do, I read firefighters' loan applications. A firefighter from the Bronx requests money to renovate his home, one from Staten Island needs money to divorce his wife, another one needs an emergency medical loan, another one declines to reveal what he needs the money for, which is a reliable way to get his loan denied but that probably also means he needs the money to pay back a gambling debt or something, according to Tommy.

After I finish filing a stack of declined pension loan applications, Dolores comes into my area and asks if she can speak to me. We walk back to her area, and I sit on a chair next to a little desk behind her desk that the office messenger sometimes sits at when there's no mail to carry, and she says, "So, you . . . you got an Apple?"

I say, "An Apple computer?"

She nods. Next to her, Tommy says, "I knew it! He looks just like that kid in the TV ads for Apples."

I laugh and nod and Dolores says, "Me and my husband just got a new Apple. I bought it for him for his birthday. But we have no idea how to work it, you know? We liked how it looked but we didn't know it's not like a regular computer." I nod and she goes on, "And we was wondering if you could come and help us set it up and show us how to work it." I smile and say, "Sure!"

Dolores clocks out early, and then after work, me and Dolores take the bus uptown, to 108th Street and Second Avenue, Tito Puente Way, and she tells me about her grandson. She says he is about my age, and he's in the army, and he's fighting in Afghanistan, and he sends her short emails sometimes. I don't know anyone who is in the military, and I feel sorry for her having to worry about him and also wonder what he's like. She says, "He's like you, you know, always with the cell phone." We pass the United Nations building and I look up at it and it looks like a big iPad. I point that out to her and she agrees. She says, "You know Henry, from IT?" I say, "Yeah, the guy who never tucks his shirt in?" She nods and says, "Yeah. He used to work here until about five or six years ago, and then he enlisted in the army and went to fight in Iraq. He got real messed up, then did some therapy, after a year or two they gave him his job back."

I say, "That's good, then," and feel bad for having pointed out that he never tucks his shirt in, which she probably already noticed but I still shouldn't have said given that he is a war veteran.

Dolores tells me about Tommy. She says he likes me and he

thinks I'm smart but he wishes I would talk to him more and hang out with him more. She says, "You know, some people in the office . . . They think, you know, because you went to college, and a lot of us didn't . . ." It's hard for her to get the words out here. "They think you think you're better than them or something, you know what I mean?"

I shake my head and say, "Everyone in the office makes more money than I do. I don't know what they're worried about." She nods and looks at me sympathetically. I go on, "Plus, like, you know I'm not like that."

We pass 57th and Sutton, and I look right and see some homeless people lounging in the little park. That seems pleasant. I imagine coming here with Alexandra sometime. Dolores smiles and says, "But you'll be making more when you're older because you went to college." I shrug and she confides, "That's why, upstairs, they're not giving you full-time work. They know you could do all the work that any of them do: the Loans counselors, Pension Payroll, anyone. And probably better. But the higher-ups think everybody would get upset if you got a promotion because everybody else here has been here longer, you know? They got seniority. And the office is real cliquey, and they think, you know, maybe this isn't the right office for you."

"I thought that might be a possibility but it doesn't really matter. I'm starting to like the office. I like working my hours as they are now. It gives me a chance to do other stuff outside work."

She says, "You got a second job?"

I say, "Sort of. I'm going to be studying for the law school entrance exam soon . . ."

She smiles and nods and says, "That's good." She feels sort of maternal to me now, and I wish we hadn't spent so much time avoiding each other.

We get off the bus and walk into Dolores's building and then take the elevator up to her apartment. She has a huge TV and some candles with stickers of Jesus on them near the windows, and her husband comes out of his bedroom and greets me. She is about four foot nine and cherubic, as I said earlier, and her husband is about six foot six and rail-thin and has leathery skin and hollow cheeks. He looks gruff. They lead me to their living room and their Mac, a MacBook laptop, and I open the screen and it seems like they haven't used it beyond entering all the new owner information. Her husband offers me a bottle of water and I take it, and then I start going through the computer with them: showing them how to control the look and feel of the computer in System Preferences, connecting to the Internet by stealing a neighbor's unsecured wireless connection without explaining that that's what I'm doing, setting up Gmail accounts and showing them how to use the camera on the front of the Mac. Dolores giggles when I take a picture of the three of us with it, and she makes me save it as her desktop background, and her husband takes meticulous notes in a marble notebook.

Dolores gets up and goes to the bathroom and her husband whispers to me, "So what if I want to look at websites that, you know" — he pauses and considers his choice of words — "Dolores wouldn't, uhhhhh . . ." I cut him off and smile and nod and show him how to turn on Private Browsing in Safari so he can look at porn.

I say, "Just make sure to quit the program when you're done." I wonder if sharing wisdom on how to hide your Internet porn is a common way for people from different generations to bond, and I suspect it is. He smiles widely and thanks me in a whisper, and then Dolores comes back from the bathroom as I am explaining iTunes.

After about an hour, Dolores says, "Okay, I think that's just about all I can learn for one day!" They ask me if I want another bottle of water and I say, "No, thank you," because if I took it I would probably have to pee on the subway, and then I put on my windbreaker and start walking toward the door. Dolores's husband says, "Wait a minute!" He goes into his bedroom and comes back with some folded-up bills and hands them to me and I say, "Oh, no, please, that's fine," and he smiles and grabs my arm and stuffs the bills into my pocket, and I thank them, and Dolores says, "See you tomorrow!" I walk out the door and take the subway downtown.

61

I pick Alexandra up at work and we walk up Hudson Street toward the L and she is silent for a few seconds.

"I got in to MacDowell," she says.

I say, "What's MacDowell?"

She says, "It's an artists' colony in New Hampshire, where they pay you to go write in a cabin for two months. It's very prestigious."

"I didn't know you applied?"

"I didn't tell anyone in case I didn't get in." I nod and think about what I am going to say next and look at a couple holding hands about forty feet ahead of us, and Alexandra sees them too, and I am silently praying that they turn a corner or something so we don't have to keep looking at them, and she continues, "Only fifteen people get in out of hundreds that apply."

"Why can't you write here? I write here and I think it's a good place to write."

"It's impossible to work on my novel after coming home at 6:30 and having to go to work at 9:30. I need the time to work so I can get something done."

"I get stuff done and I work."

She doesn't say anything.

I say to her, weakly, "Can you not leave?" I look at her face and it is unmoving, and she says she has to leave, but that she'll be back in two months and I can come visit while she is there, but only once and I can never come into her cabin because that's against the rules. I don't know why it feels like such a big deal for her to leave for two months if I can visit, but I think it's because she'll meet someone who's a better match for her and sleep with him.

She says, "I don't want to be a bad investment anymore. I'm older than you. It's not as fun at this age."

"People in New York sometimes don't make money until they're forty! They always look like they're having a good time."

She smiles and says, "It's probably even less fun at that age."

I am resigned, so I say, "When would you go?"

She says, "Two weeks." She says she's sorry and tries to kiss me but I pull away. She says, very slowly and tenderly and sadly, with a lilt at the end, "Honey . . ." I shake my head.

We take the L train home in silence except sometimes she moves her head close to mine and makes meowing noises and she puts her head on my shoulder because she wants me to not be upset with her, but I can't not be upset with her so I move my shoulder. She touches my hand and I pull it away. She shouldn't leave me alone in New York for two months with no sexual outlet, and no partner to go swimming in the river with and to bounce ideas off, and no girlfriend to go to parties with in case I get invited to any cool parties.

When the train gets to her subway stop, we hug and she gets up and gets off the train.

62

Later that night I come home and Mike and Ian and an unidentified cute girl with red hair are watching *Seinfeld* on Mike's laptop on the coffee table in the living room and smoking a joint.
I look at the joint and point to it and I say, "Who rolled that?
That looks perfect." The girl raises her hand and giggles, and I
say, "Bravo." Ian says, "We also took Ambiens. You want some?"

"Will I definitely hallucinate?"

"If you stay awake."

"Okay."

Ian gives me two Ambiens so I take one of them, and then
before its effects set in, I talk about Alexandra going to Mac-
Dowell, and I say, "I understand that Alexandra's career and success as a writer is more important than anything to her, including me, but if she really needs to write, if she's really born to
write and destined to be a writer and everything, shouldn't she
be able to do it from anywhere and do anything necessary to
do it?" Ian and Mike and the red-haired girl look at me in con-
fusion, I guess because they're incapacitated. I sit down on the
arm of the couch and try to watch *Seinfeld* with them.

Ian says, "Can I be honest for a second?" I nod and he says, "It
doesn't seem like you even really like her . . ."

I say, "I don't, like, *love* her. But I'd still prefer if she didn't
leave. I guess thinking about both being alone and her being

with someone else bothers me more than thinking about not being with her . . ."

I stumble into my room and there is a text from Emma on my phone: "I am visiting New York soon. Can I see you?" I text her back, "Maybe, probably not, have girlfriend, sorry, don't trust myself, not at liberty to see you unless I don't have girlfriend by then," and then lie down in bed and fall asleep with my clothes on. When I wake up the next morning, she has texted me back and it says, "I have a boyfriend. I just wanted to talk."

63

A week later, Alexandra comes over and we watch *Resident Evil 2* in bed, at my request, and eat Utz chips while we watch. There is a possibility that we will have sex tonight, and I think we both feel a responsibility to have sex with the other, but neither of us is interested enough in initiating it to make it happen.

In the middle of the movie she announces that she's tired. We finish the movie and I get a smaller bag of chips from the kitchen and bring it back to bed. Alexandra uses her laptop.

I am gaining weight, but I don't care yet because it's not enough weight where I feel like I have reached the threshold of visible weight gain. It is a small weight gain that only I know about, maybe Alexandra a little bit, but if I keep eating bags of chips like this, other people might start to notice. I wonder if my chip intake is diminishing her sexual appetite, but even if it is, I don't think that's what's at the heart of what's happening.

I take my laptop off my nightstand and lie on the inside of the bed, next to the window, and check my email. There are a lot of spam emails from people doing PR for indie bands who want me to write about the bands they are promoting. There are no writing job offers and no new fan emails, so I take the opportunity to respond to an old fan letter whose subject line is, "Writing to You From A Pit of Despair," and the body is a four-thousand-word confessional about the author stealing money from her parents. I wonder if the person even reads my blog anymore.

After I check my email, I read new postings in an anonymous message board about my blog. The message board has about 1,500 posts about my blog, all under anonymous handles, and the people on the message board write about me like there is no chance I would ever come across their posts. One of the posters writes, "I think there is probably a degree of Asperger's syndrome at work with this kid," and then another poster confirms that diagnosis and copies and pastes a short Wikipedia summary of the symptoms of Asperger's into the message board and posts that. Other posters agree.

I close my laptop and get out of bed and put a shirt on and Alexandra says, "Where are you going?" I say, "I'm going to call my dad and ask him if I have Asperger's. People on a message board are saying I have it." Alexandra laughs and says, "Honey, come on, think about what you do! You probably do have a little Asperger's. It's cute. You wouldn't be the same without it." I walk out into the living room and look out the window and call my dad.

It's about 11:30 at night and he picks up and I can hear an Internet talk radio show playing in the background. "Hey, Dad," I say. "How's it going?"

He says, "How it's going? Down the tubes. Do you understand?" He lingers on the word "understand," and then goes on, "And there's nothing we can do about it beside protect ourselves. Why don't you ask me how Mr. G is doing? Mr. G is going to three thousand, five thousand, twenty thousand! Are you not learning? Do you not trust your father?" I don't ever interrupt him during his opening tirade because it only spurs more tirades. The best strategy is to just refocus him early in the conversation, so I say, "Dad, no, I mean, like . . . How is your evening going?"

He thinks for a second and inhales and then exhales and says, "I am fine. Mom made lasagna but she put too much salt." He thinks again and says, "Why do you call so late?"

I say, "Someone said that I have Asperger's and I wanted to know what you thought of that diagnosis."

My dad thinks for a second and laughs a little bit and says, "Boy, I don't think you have this. Maybe you do, but it doesn't interfere with your life, so I don't worry. If you want to know for sure, I would have to conduct a fuller diagnosis, and I can't do it over the phone in a minute or a few minutes." He thinks for a second and then says, playfully, "But I think you really have a *loch in kop*," meaning a hole in the head in Yiddish or German. He laughs after he says this too. I guess it's difficult for any parent to admit that there is something up with their child's mental health, even if there is, so I drop the issue.

I say, "Okay, cool, thanks. That's all I wanted to ask."

"Are you sleeping now? It's late."

"Yeah, I'm about to go to sleep. I have work in the morning." He makes a grunting sound to indicate that he understands, and then I say, "Did you ever get a chance to read that *Times* article about my blog from July?"

He thinks for a second and says, "Yes, boy. Very good."

"Did you understand it? I know the whole thing is kind of complicated."

"I know . . . You write about the music, but, you know, this is not my field, so I don't understand in the same way as someone your age. Mom tried to explain to me, but, ehhhh, you know . . ."

I smile and say, "Okay, thank you for reading it."

I know what's coming next because now I owe him one. He says, "Did you watch the YouTube about the Irish debt?"

"Yeah, I watched it the day you sent it. It was really interesting."

"Did you read the Alex Jones article I sent also? About the Irish debt?"

"Yes." I didn't actually read or watch either of those things, but he rarely quizzes me on them, but I'd still prefer not to lie to him all the time, so I tell him I watch and read just the minimum amount of the things he sends me so that he will be satisfied with my adherence to his dogma and not stop authorizing the payment of my rent. Sometimes I think that he doesn't really care that I am reading the actual text or watching the actual video, just doing something he says, because I'm his only son. He says, "Good boy," and then he hangs up.

I come back to bed and Alexandra lies next to me and listens to NPR on headphones and edits a story for *Granta*. I think that she couldn't possibly be that tired if she's editing. I put my hand on her thigh, near her vagina, and she wiggles her hips away and whispers, "I can't, I'm editing."

I think, "We are too young to not have sex, even if we don't like each other that much." I read some old Pitchfork interviews and think about what I am going to write tomorrow. It is not as easy to think about stuff to write about after having written hundreds of thousands of words about Pitchfork, and I feel like I'm scraping the bottom of the barrel of my ideas, but I hope that readers aren't noticing, and I don't think they are because my posts are getting more and more Notes, generally. But some days I will write a post and it does not get as many

Notes as the post I wrote the day before, and I will walk home and think nervously about it, like, "Am I out of good ideas? Are people over this whole thing and the novelty of reading reviews of Pitchfork reviews has worn off? What happens when I can't think of anything to write about? This is the only thing I can really do."

64

Alexandra falls asleep and I am having trouble falling asleep so I take the other Ambien that Ian gave me and root around on the Internet for something to read. I click on my Gmail tab and look at everyone on Gchat, but I don't see anyone I want to chat with. I look over at Alexandra and she's sleeping, and I pick my phone up and turn it slightly away from Alexandra and text Emma, "I miss you." I look out the window and think about what Emma is doing, and then my thoughts start to feel a little mushy and I know the Ambien is working.

The next morning I wake up and my laptop is open on my lap next to a half-eaten bag of chips, and my glasses are still on, and Alexandra is gone because she went to work, and I go over to my desk and plug my laptop in and read one of the conversations I apparently had with a Pitchfork writer on Google Chat last night, which I don't remember because of the Ambien. At 1:32 A.M., I wrote, "katie. i'm in my bed on ambien. i have a loose grasp of reality." Katie didn't respond so I continued, "my head feels like someone just ran warm water through it to filter the brains or irrigate them, like bathing brains in warm water. this would be like taking them to the spa. do you understand?" Katie didn't respond again so I continued, "okay i see you are busy now so i won't bother more. let's talk soon when i'm less like this."

65

Alexandra leaves for MacDowell and I come with her to the Port Authority to say good-bye. She wears a black coat and skinny black jeans and a sweater. She buys her bus ticket and I carry her bag to the terminal, and we stand there for a while, in the basement of the bus station, looking at the people walking past us. I reach down to hold her hand and she holds my hand for a second and then pulls her hand away and I look at her quizzically and she says, "Your hand is really dry, you need moisturizer."

"Do you have any moisturizer?" I ask.

"It's packed really deep in my bag . . ."

"You can't hold my hand unless I put on moisturizer?"

"I'd prefer not to, it's so dry, you know, it's scaly. It's because it's winter."

I lean over to her and whisper very calmly and sternly, and so other people around us won't hear this, "Honestly, listen. I am your boyfriend, you just *need* to hold my hand."

She looks at me in surprise. I whisper, "I'm sorry, but saying you won't hold my hand because it's 'too dry' is so weird. We are supposed to like each other, and people who really like each other hold hands no matter how dry their hands are. Your hand is sweaty a lot and I hold it when it's sweaty." I reach down and grasp Alexandra's hand and she lets me but hers is limp. She looks defiant. After about a minute, she grasps my hand back and says, "I'm sorry too. You're right." I kiss her on the hair.

A group of black people dressed in religious garb walks by and we try to figure out what religion they belong to. "Muslims?" Alexandra says.

"I think they could be Christians too."

"Will you definitely come visit me?"

"If I can."

"Why wouldn't you be able to come?" I think about how if Emma comes back to New York and wants to be with me, I would do that, but then I say, "I don't know. I can't foresee anything coming up but, like, what if someone in my family dies or something?"

"There are like seven people in your family."

"Yeah, I know, and all of them are old." We stand there looking at people walk past us.

I say, "Do you know anyone else who's going to be up there at the same time as you?" She thinks for a second and says, "Yeah, this guy Mark who was in my grad program." I know her grad program was very small and everyone knew each other. I want to say, "Tell me about your sexual history with Mark, who you will be spending two months in isolated cabins with," but I don't, because if she tells me she has no sexual history with him I probably wouldn't believe her, and if she happens to say it in the most convincing possible way and I do believe her, it won't matter anyway because people don't need to have had sex in the past to have sex in the future, especially when they are in cabins in the woods together for two months and their boyfriends aren't around. Especially when they have boyfriends they are willing to leave for two months to work on their writing, which can be done from anywhere.

If she tells me she does have a sexual history with him but there's nothing between them now, I almost definitely won't believe her because if you've agreed to have sex with somebody in the past, you will almost definitely be willing, given the right circumstances, to have sex with them again, unless they've done something monstrous to you.

I try to think of the person who I have had sex with who I would want to have sex with least right now, and I imagine having sex with her and I know I would do it again. She has very short hair now, so it wouldn't be ideal given my preference in women's hair length, but it could occur physically. Alexandra looks at her bus pulling in, and we kiss and she walks out to the bus. I wave to her through a window in the basement of the Port Authority as she slides into her bus seat and opens a book.

66

A week after Alexandra leaves, I'm at work and there is nothing to do so I go and sit in the chair near Dolores's desk. She asks me if I am close with my parents and I say, "Sort of. We get along. I think they're disappointed that I haven't done anything with my life yet."

She smiles and says, "You're only twenty-two though!"

I say, "My dad was in medical school when he was twenty-two."

She says, "Are you seeing, you know . . ." She tries to think of the appropriate pronoun to allow for the fact that she's not positive about my sexual orientation and doesn't want to offend me, and she continues, ". . . anybody right now?"

"Yeah, I have a girlfriend."

Tommy looks over at me and goes, "*You* got a girlfriend?"

I nod, and Dolores says to Tommy, "Shush!" Then she looks at me and says, "He's just jealous because he don't have a girlfriend."

Tommy says, "Come on, I got plenty of girls," and Dolores says, "Yeah, you meet them all at bars! Where you just get them drunk! That's not a real woman, that's a floozy!" Dolores laughs.

Tommy looks demure and says, quietly, "Plenty of good girls too, though." Dolores ignores this and turns back to me and I say, "We've been dating for about six months."

Dolores says, "What does she do?"

I say, "She's at an artists' colony in New Hampshire right now," and Tommy starts laughing and we both look at him and he points at me and says, "YO, YOUR GIRLFRIEND IS AT A *NUDIST* COLONY?! HOW'D YOU LET THAT HAPPEN?!"

Dolores tells him to shush again and he finishes laughing and says, "Nah, nah, I'm playin', I'm playin.'" Then Eileen from Legal brings down a stack of papers, divorce decrees, and plops them in front of Dolores, who has to enter her receipt of the papers into the computer before Tommy carries them back to my desk so I can file them. Dolores starts entering them into the system, and then Tommy looks at me and says, "Yo, NYU, me and Hector, the custodian, we going for some burgers after work — you wanna grab some burgers?"

"I get off at two thirty and you guys get off at six so I don't know if that would be possible. I'm sorry, I would like to come." I'm not sure I would really like to come, but I don't want Tommy to know that.

"Oh yeah, that's right. Aight, next time."

67

A week later, I'm lying in my bed with my laptop on my stomach and Gchatting with Alexandra and she says she has to get back to work. I say, "Okay, see you later, honey," and she signs off. I get up and go into the kitchen and pour myself a cup of vodka and sip it and walk back into my room.

I get a request to be added to another Gchat user's chat list, and the email address is Emma's name. I accept the request and Emma pops up in my Gchat list, and it is almost like seeing her for the first time in seven months. I look at her name and I think about her hair and can remember how it smells. A chat message pops up on my screen and it says, "hi."

I write back, "hi," and Emma says, "how are you doing?" I say, "i'm okay. my girlfriend is at an artists' colony and i am running out of ideas for my blog, but besides that all okay. how are you?"

She says, "i'm okay too. my contract is almost over and i don't really like it here."

I say, "what are you going to do when your contract is over?"

I am hopeful that the next thing she says will be "come back to New York" or "you."

But instead she says, "i need to work and make money."

"you could come back to New York and live with your family and find a job?"

"i think living with my parents would be worse than almost anything."

I say, "i think you could find a job here and move out of your parents' apartment pretty quickly," and then I say, "do you still have a boyfriend?"

She says, "yeah."

"tell me about him."

"his name is brian. he's a mountain man, like he likes climbing and fishing and being outdoors."

I try to think about something negative you could say about someone who is outdoorsy, which seems to be a universally positive quality.

"sounds like a real intellectual."

I look over at the Venus flytrap and water it with the water in the cup on my windowsill.

She replies, "hahaha, no, he's sweet though."

I say, "do you actually like him? or is he just, like, there?"

She says, "at first he was just here, but i've grown to like him."

I say, "i've grown to like kale but that doesn't mean i want to sleep with it."

She says, "why are you being weird? i miss you too but there are normal ways to express that."

I say, "i don't know, i know, i feel crazy right now. remember when you told me to start my Tumblr? it has 15,000 followers now. how many followers does the mountain man's Tumblr have? does he tumbl all the way down the mountain?"

She writes back, "good for you," and "haha . . ." Then she says, "this is an ugly side of you." I don't really know what to say here. It is an ugly side of me.

I say, "so you're coming back to New York after your contract is finished?" She doesn't reply. I look over at the Venus flytrap and realize that I just watered it with vodka. I sit there and wait. The screen says, "Emma is typing," and then "Emma has entered text," and then "Emma is typing again."

Emma says, "we really shouldn't be having conversations like this."

I say, "i know, but it feels nice to talk to you."

"it makes me upset to talk to you. i don't know why i gchatted you."

"upset in a good way?"

"i don't know what you mean."

"like, upset in a nostalgic and tender way?"

"maybe a little of that, but also upset in a conventional way."

I ignore this and say, "can you come back to new york after your contract is over please?" She doesn't reply. I sit there and wait for a reply. The screen says, "Emma is typing," and then "Emma has entered text." I look at my desk and she doesn't reply, and then I look at an empty can of beer on the floor and she still doesn't reply. Then she replies, "i am staying out here indefinitely. i'm just getting a different job. this is where i live now."

68

On the bus trip up to visit Alexandra at MacDowell, I sit next to an ugly and probably stupid person and read a collection of zines published as a book. I work on coming up with ideas for posts for the upcoming week, which become worse and worse as my original well of ideas is dry. I fidget and adjust in my seat, and then someone from a magazine emails me to say they want to interview me over the phone.

I email them back to ask for their phone number, go into my phone's settings and change them so that my own phone number is blocked on the Caller ID of the person who I am calling so I appear mysterious and anonymous, and make the call. The person from the magazine asks me a few astute questions and then a few questions that make me think that they don't really understand my writing, but I try to be as polite as possible to them so they don't selectively quote me and make me look bad.

As I'm answering questions in the interview, a middle-aged man sitting in the row behind me who was apparently sleeping taps me on the shoulder with a newspaper to get me to quiet down, and I turn back and look at him with irritation and nod. Then the guy on the other end of the phone says, "Where are you?" I lean my chair back a few inches, hoping the man behind me realizes that I am within my rights to do so and he has no recourse to address his newly diminished amount of legroom, and I say, "I'm on a bus on my way to visit my girlfriend at an artists' colony."

"Oh, that sounds cool, are you excited?"

"Please don't print this in the interview, but no."

He laughs and says he won't print it, and then he asks me some more questions and we get off the phone.

69

Alexandra picks me up at the bus station in Peterborough and looks like she is trying to be excited to see me. We haven't spoken much in the last month because we don't have very much to say to each other, and it's nighttime, and it's cold out, and she kisses me and we walk out of the bus station and down the long road toward the town next to where the artists' colony is. She explains to me again that it is against the rules of the artists' colony for any noncolony members to enter any of the cabins, and I think about whether any other colony members have entered her cabin, and then she says, "We'll be staying in a motel in Peterborough and that will be just as fun." She sounds like a consoling mom in a movie about a disappointing family vacation.

I ask her how her work is coming and she says that she has 25,000 words of a novel, which she won't tell me anything about, which I figure means it's about other guys, and it is coming along beautifully, and I tell her I am happy to hear that. We walk through eerily quiet streets lined with small suburban houses, and I think about how I don't like being here because it's too quiet and empty.

"Where are all the people?"

"Inside their houses, probably sleeping."

I say, "I don't like being in areas that aren't densely populated. It encourages crime."

"You sound like you're trying to sound like Woody Allen."

I ignore this and say, "Like, if you think of the archetypal urban mugging, it always occurs in an empty back-alley, not on a crowded street with tons of people around to see the criminal."

We get closer to town and walk past a convenience store and I say, "I'm going inside to get some beer because I just spent eight hours on a bus. Do you want anything?" She shakes her head and I buy four 24 oz. cans of Bud Light Lime.

"What'd you get?" Alexandra asks when I come out of the store.

"Bud Light Limes."

"Those are gross! That's like putting Diet Sprite in beer."

"Yeah, but they're, like, *fun* beers."

"How are they fun? They don't taste as good as almost any other beer, and they're full of chemicals with twenty-letter names. Neither of those things are fun."

"People who drink these are always having fun. Like, think about the things people do when they're drinking different drinks: people who are drinking tequila are partying and dancing and acting wild, people drinking whiskey and gin might be more down-tempo and might be crying, people drinking vodka can be doing pretty much whatever because vodka doesn't really have an identity."

Alexandra looks at me quizzically so I continue, to reinforce my point, "Envision a really sad old man who is sitting at the end of a dark, cobwebby bar with an old jukebox and neon signs advertising beers like Schlitz and Pabst all around, some really sad old soul song is playing on the jukebox, and the old man is rubbing his fingers across his forehead and he's crying because his wife just left him or something, and then you look at the drink he's drinking and you see it's a bright green can of Bud Light Lime. It would be an absurd image, right?" Alexandra smiles and nods. I continue, "People drinking Bud Light Limes are partying and having a good time, like with Coronas."

"Why didn't you get Corona Lights?"

"More calories."

70

We check into a motel in town and go up to our room, and then Alexandra gets a phone call so she goes outside to take it, and I try to think about who would be calling her, and then she comes back inside and says, "It was Lexi, he just had a question about when *Granta* comes out." I nod and we lie down in bed and watch an inning of a Yankees game while I drink a Bud Light Lime. It's tense. Alexandra looks over at me and says, "Do you have to drink to want to be with me?"

"I want to be with you almost all of the time, except when we're fighting," which used to be more true than it is now.

"Stop doing that."

"Stop doing what?"

"Being obstinately literal. You know what I meant. I meant, do you have to drink to want to have sex with me?" I shake my head.

"Can you stop drinking then?" I nod and put the Bud Light Lime down on the table next to the bed and then I roll over next to her and we make out for about forty-five seconds and then start taking our clothes off, and then we have sex for the first time in a month, and then we put our clothes back on and walk down the road to the McDonald's, where I get a fish sandwich.

On our walk back to the motel from the McDonald's, I tell myself that I should really try to make it work with Alexandra because I don't have any prospects outside of her right now, and so I would be choosing between sex and no sex. I feel like she's thinking the same thing about me. I wish I had spent some time cultivating a farm team.

Then we get back to the hotel and finish watching the game. The Yankees win and Mike texts me, "Yanks won." I write back, "I know, I watched."

He writes back, "Aren't you at mcdowell? Do they have TVs in the cabins?"

"Not allowed into the cabins."

71

Two days later, on a cold and cloudy afternoon, Alexandra walks me back to the bus station and we get there and wait for my bus and I kiss her on the hair and I sniff because I have a little dust or something in my nose, and I notice that her hair smells a little bit. She looks up at me and goes, "Does my hair smell?"

"No, honey, it doesn't smell."

"I feel like you just made a sniffing noise near my hair that makes me think it smells. Does it smell?"

"No."

"Really, just be honest with me and tell me if it smells. I know you think it smells and I just want you to be honest with me and tell me the truth, no matter what it is." I look at her hair and she says, slowly with an eerie calmness that borders on a primal challenge, "So. Does it smell?"

I think very carefully about what I am going to say here, as I try to do always but sometimes forget to do. I play out the possible scenarios of how she will react based on my answer choices, I think about how to choose my words beyond just a simple yes or no, I think about what I am even doing here, and I see my bus pulling up into the parking lot out of the corner of my eye.

And then I say, timidly, "Yeah, like just a tiny bit? Did you shampoo today? It could just be because of that if you didn't?"

She says, "Why didn't you just say that when I asked you the first time?"

"Because you might have flipped out," I say.

My bus pulls up in front of us. She looks at the bus and then back at me and says, "I wouldn't have flipped out. I'm not fucking crazy." Then I kiss her and tell her I'll see her in a month and good luck on the novel, and then I get back onto the bus and it pulls away and takes me, mercifully, back to New York City. But then, while I'm waiting for my subway in the Port Authority, I think about how depressing it would be to be alone again.

72

I go home and ask Mike to use his Facebook password, and he asks me why I want it, and I tell him just to see if there are any pictures of me on there from college that I haven't seen because I don't have Facebook. He shrugs and gives me his password, and then I walk into my room and close the door behind me and go on Emma's Facebook and look at pictures of her with her new boyfriend, who is taller than me and has a blocky head. Then I find some pictures of her without her boyfriend and masturbate and lie in bed for a while, looking at the Venus flytrap that I killed, and then I go into the kitchen and get a bag of chips and eat them while streaming *Seinfeld* and falling asleep.

73

The day before Alexandra comes back from MacDowell, I sit at my desk in the file room and finish grinding through four reviews of the day's Pitchfork reviews and send my post to Mike and then start writing my second post of the day. I start writing something about the Hold Steady, and it sounds stupid so I erase it and then try to start over.

Then, nothing comes to me like it has on every single day, excluding weekends, for the last eight or so months. I search and search and then nothing is coming, and I go into my BlackBerry MemoPad and look up saved ideas for posts, but none of those brief ideas seem like they could be turned into anything worth reading. I think, "If any of those ideas were worth anything, I would have turned them into posts already." I look around at the filing boxes and the microfiche and the yellowing typewriters, the fluorescent light above me with dead bugs trapped in it, and nothing comes. If this were a different era, I would be tapping a pencil against my desk and then my temple.

I start to panic and call Mike and he picks up and I say, "Hey, I don't have any ideas for an afternoon post! What do I write about?" He says, "Man, I don't know, it's your blog. I don't think the way you need to think to write that. It's so personal, you know?" I call Alexandra and she doesn't pick up because she is working and maybe out of service inside a cabin in the woods.

I wait an hour and frantically try to think of something to write about, but it seems like the harder I think, the further away an idea becomes. I file some loan applications. I talk to Dolores and Tommy about the weather. I think about whether I could keep writing about Pitchfork reviews exclusively in my blog, without writing the personal and other music stuff that I loved writing about, but then I say something in my head that I have been thinking for a long time but have never said to myself, which is I don't really care that much about taking down Pitchfork anymore because the guys who work there are just some other dweebs like me. What else is there left to say?

I walk back to my desk and start composing an email to Mike, for him to post on my blog, and it goes, "Hi! I am going to go away for a while to generate new ideas. Someday I will be back because I like blogging, but not now." Then I think about sending it for a while, but I decide not to because if people don't think of me as a blogger, then what will they think of me as? Nobody even knows what I do for a living and some of my best friends, like Lexi, don't even know my real name. Being a blogger is my whole thing. I sit at my desk and think about my future and hope that tomorrow or later today I will be able to come up with another idea, and then another few ideas, and then a stream of ideas that will make people want to keep reading my blog, but I don't know if I can.

I finish work and take the subway home, and when I get out of the subway, I get four emails from people that all say something like, "Is there something up with my browser or did you not post today? What's the deal, man?" I don't write back to any of them but it's nice to know they're out there. It is January 15, and my Tumblr has 32,564 followers, which I suspect is somewhere near the most followers it will ever have, and I try to make peace with the fact that I will no longer be receiving substantial attention from people who I will never see or meet, but it's hard.

After I read those four emails, I call my mom on her cell phone and she picks up and says, "David? Are you okay?"

I say, "Yeah, why would I not be okay?"

"You didn't put anything up on your blog today. I got worried."

"You read my blog every day? I thought you just wanted to know the address, like, to have it on file." She says, "No, I read it every day. I like reading it." She pauses and goes on, "Partially because you're my only son and I want to know what you're doing and thinking at every moment and make sure you're safe and happy." She laughs self-consciously and goes on, "I was learning a lot about you from it, you know?" She says, with a drop of sadness in her voice, "Why don't you ever talk to me and Dad the way you write to people on your blog?"

"I don't know . . . ? I guess, in a way, it's just easier to be honest with people you don't know than people who your words affect."

She thinks for a second and says, "Maybe that's a generational thing?"

"Yeah, maybe. I'm not going to write it anymore for a while, maybe not ever. I just don't have any more ideas for what to write about."

"Does it have to do with the *Times* article?"

"Why would it have to do with that?"

"Maybe being put in the spotlight made you feel more pressure?"

"No, I don't think so. Maybe."

"So, back to my original question: Are you okay?"

"Yeah, mostly. I'll live."

Two hours later my dad calls, and he says, "Duvie! Mom said you ended your website? Is this true?"

"Well, I didn't exactly end it, but yeah, sort of. It just felt over. I'm out of ideas."

"Mom says she thinks it may be because of your father? Because we tell you to do law school? She says, 'Maybe he doesn't want to do law school? Why do we force him?' Is this true? Do you not want to do law school?"

"No, I do," I say. "I just need to be ready to want to do it, you know?"

"You don't have to do if you don't want. You find something else."

"I appreciate that, but I want to." I think for a second and say, "So would you want to come see my apartment? I've been living here for a while and you're paying for it so you should at least come check it out, like at least to see if you're getting ripped off."

He laughs and says, "In Brooklyn? It's dirty! Too loud." I laugh and say, "Okay, I understand."

74

Alexandra comes back from MacDowell and I meet her at her apartment. She sits outside on the stoop smoking a Parliament Light and I sit down next to her and kiss her cheek and take a cigarette out of her pack and light it. It's cloudy and below freezing outside and there's a thin layer of snow and ice on the ground. The wind stings my eyes.

"How's it going, honey?"

"David, I can't do this anymore." I wish she would at least wait until we got inside.

"Why not?"

"I think I just need to be by myself right now, you know?"

"Did you meet someone at MacDowell? Or before Mac-Dowell and then, you know, slept with them at MacDowell?" She shakes her head and I look closely at her face to see if she's telling the truth.

I say, "Is it because I stopped writing my blog?"

"You stopped writing your blog?"

I get up, and I'm nodding, and I say good-bye and I walk home and it starts to snow. I feel despondent about being alone. I think about having to meet someone new again and then learning her birthday and how she smells and the kind of beer she prefers, and tucking my shirt in to meet her parents, and then another one after that and then another one after that, and then the looming possibility beyond, which is that I will get older and never meet someone who I won't break up with or who won't break up with me. I listen to "The Fox in the Snow" by Belle and Sebastian, and then when it ends, I listen to it over and over again until I get home.